Shadows of a Perfect Life

Shane Reed

Copyright

Copyright © 2024 by Shane Reed
All rights reserved.

Chapter 1

The steering wheel creaked under Robert Langdon's white-knuckled grip as he sat motionless in his parked car. His jaw clenched, eyes fixed on the looming Victorian house before him - his childhood home, now a monument to unmet expectations.

"You can do this," he muttered, trying to summon some hidden reserve of courage. But the pep talk rang hollow, drowned out by his mother's imagined criticisms echoing in his mind.

Robert's gaze drifted to the dashboard clock: 2:47 PM. His heart rate quickened. Mother would be home from her garden club meeting in precisely 13 minutes.

"Damn it," he hissed, thumping the wheel in frustration. He'd wasted too much time second-guessing himself. Now the window for action was rapidly closing.

Taking a deep breath, Robert closed his eyes and tried to center himself. The leather seat creaked as he shifted, bringing a whiff of the car's new-car smell - a scent that usually filled him with pride, but now only reminded him of his mother's disdain for such "frivolous purchases."

"Focus, Robert," he said aloud, his voice barely above a whisper. "You're not that scared little boy anymore. You're a grown man. You can handle this."

But even as the words left his lips, doubt crept in. Could he really go through with his plan? Was he prepared to face the consequences?

The dashboard clock now read 2:49. Time was slipping away.

"It's now or never," Robert muttered, steeling himself for what lay ahead. He took one final deep breath, filling his lungs with resolve. Whatever happened next, there was no turning back now.

Robert's hand flew to the door handle, yanking it open with a sudden burst of determination. He stepped out, his polished oxfords meeting the pavement with a sharp click that echoed through the quiet suburban street. Each stride towards the house felt both impossibly long and far too quick, his heart pounding in sync with his footfalls.

The manicured lawn and meticulously pruned rosebushes seemed to mock him, their perfection a stark reminder of the relentless expectations that had haunted him since childhood. Robert's eyes locked onto the familiar red door, its brass knocker glinting in the afternoon sun.

As he reached the porch, his confident facade faltered. His hand, poised to ring the doorbell, trembled slightly. Robert hesitated, a war of emotions playing across his features.

"Come on, you coward," he muttered to himself, his voice barely audible. "It's just a house. It's just a conversation."

But it wasn't just a house, was it? And it certainly wouldn't be just a conversation. This moment, this decision, held the weight of years of pent-up resentment and unfulfilled expectations.

Robert's finger hovered over the doorbell, a hair's breadth away from pressing it. He swallowed hard, his throat suddenly dry. "What if..." he began, then shook his head, banishing the thought. "No. No more 'what ifs.' It's time to end this charade."

With a deep breath, he steadied his hand, ready to ring the bell and face whatever lay beyond that red door. The internal conflict that had plagued him for so long crystallized into a single moment of choice.

The door swung open before Robert could ring the bell, revealing Evelyn Langdon. Her silver hair was impeccably styled, and her posture radiated authority. For a fleeting moment, her stern expression softened as she laid eyes on her son.

"Robert," she said, her voice a mix of surprise and something unreadable. With a curt nod, she stepped aside. "Come in."

Robert crossed the threshold, the familiar scent of lemon furniture polish and his mother's perfume washing over him. He glanced around the immaculate foyer, noting that nothing had changed since his last visit.

"I wasn't expecting you," Evelyn remarked, leading him into the living room. "To what do I owe this... surprise?"

Robert's jaw tightened. "Can't a son visit his mother without an agenda?"

Evelyn's eyebrow arched. "Of course. Though it's unlike you to drop by unannounced. Especially given your... current situation."

"My current situation?" Robert echoed, fighting to keep his tone neutral. "And what situation would that be, Mother?"

"Well, dear," Evelyn said, settling into her favorite armchair, "I heard about the merger falling through. Such a shame. It could have been quite the feather in your cap."

Robert's hands clenched at his sides. "The merger wasn't right for the company. Sometimes, the best deals are the ones you don't make."

Evelyn sighed, a sound laden with disappointment. "Always an excuse, Robert. When will you learn to seize opportunities instead of letting them slip away?"

Robert felt a familiar knot forming in his stomach. He'd rehearsed this conversation a hundred times in his head, but now, face-to-face with his mother, the words seemed to evaporate.

"I didn't come here to discuss business, Mother," he managed, his voice strained.

"No?" Evelyn's gaze was piercing. "Then why are you here, Robert? To reassure me that you're finally getting your life on track? That you're living up to your potential?"

Robert's carefully constructed composure began to crack. "My life is on track," he insisted, though the words sounded hollow even to his own ears. "I'm successful, I'm-"

"Successful?" Evelyn interjected, her tone sharp. "Is that what you call it? A string of missed opportunities and half-hearted attempts?"

As his mother's words cut through him, Robert felt a surge of defiance. He'd come here with a purpose, and he wouldn't let her derail him. Not this time.

Robert's jaw clenched, his teeth grinding as he fought to maintain his composure. The living room, once a sanctuary of childhood memories, now felt suffocating. Sunlight streaming through the bay window seemed to mock the darkness swirling within him.

"I've built a successful career, Mother," he said, his voice tight. "I'm respected in my field. Isn't that enough?"

Evelyn's lips pursed, her disapproval palpable. "Respected? By whom? Those who settle for mediocrity?"

Each word was a dagger, reopening old wounds Robert had desperately tried to heal. He ran a hand through his hair, disheveling the carefully styled locks.

"Why can't you ever just be proud of me?" he asked, hating the pleading note in his voice.

"Oh, Robert," Evelyn sighed, her tone softening slightly but still tinged with disappointment. "I want to be. But you have so much potential. You could be exceptional, if only you'd apply yourself."

Robert's chest tightened, a familiar mix of anger and shame bubbling up inside him. He wanted to lash out, to defend himself, but the words stuck in his throat. The urge to please her, ingrained since childhood, warred with his desire for independence.

"I am applying myself," he muttered, more to himself than to her. "Just not in the way you want."

Evelyn's eyes narrowed. "What was that?"

Robert hesitated, torn between confrontation and retreat. The ticking of the antique grandfather clock in the corner seemed to grow louder, marking each moment of indecision.

Robert's jaw clenched as he met his mother's gaze. "I said, I am applying myself. Just not in the way you want me to."

Evelyn's eyebrows arched. "Oh? And what way is that, Robert? Squandering your talents on trivial pursuits?"

"They're not trivial," Robert shot back, his voice rising. "My work matters. I've made a difference in people's lives."

"A difference?" Evelyn scoffed. "You could be changing the world, Robert. Instead, you're content with... what? Small victories?"

Robert's hands balled into fists at his sides. "Those 'small victories' mean everything to the people I help. Why can't you see that?"

"Because I see what you could be!" Evelyn's voice cracked slightly, a rare show of emotion. "You're capable of so much more."

Robert's throat tightened, a familiar ache settling in his chest. He wanted to make her understand, to break free from the suffocating weight of her expectations. But as he looked at her, he saw the determination in her eyes, the unyielding belief that she knew best.

Suddenly, something shifted inside him. The constant need for approval, the endless cycle of disappointment – it all felt hollow. Robert straightened his shoulders, a newfound resolve hardening his features.

"You're right, Mother," he said, his voice steady. "I am capable of more. But it's time I decided what that means for myself."

Evelyn's eyes widened, sensing the change in her son. "Robert, what are you saying?"

But Robert had already made up his mind. He could see the path forward clearly now, a way to break free from his mother's influence once and for all. The thought both terrified and exhilarated him.

"I'm saying goodbye, Mother," he said softly, his eyes reflecting a mix of sadness and determination. "For now, at least. It's time I lived my life on my own terms."

Robert turned away from his mother's stunned expression, striding towards the front door. The weight of his decision pressed down on him, but with each step, he felt a strange sense of lightness growing in his chest.

As he pulled open the heavy oak door, the cool evening air rushed in, carrying with it the scent of freshly cut grass and the promise of change. Robert paused for a moment, his hand on the doorknob, and looked back at Evelyn.

"I'll be in touch," he said, his voice softer now. "But I need some time."

Without waiting for a response, Robert stepped out into the night. The door clicked shut behind him, the sound echoing with a sense of finality. He took a deep breath, filling his lungs with the crisp air, and began walking towards his car.

His footsteps crunched on the gravel driveway, each one more purposeful than the last. As he approached his sleek black sedan, Robert's mind raced with possibilities. The plan he'd been mulling over for weeks now seemed not just possible, but necessary.

"It's time," he muttered to himself, fishing his keys out of his pocket. "No more living in her shadow."

As he slid into the driver's seat, Robert caught a glimpse of himself in the rearview mirror. His eyes gleamed with a mix of excitement and trepidation. He started the engine, the low purr matching the thrum of anticipation in his veins.

Pulling out of the driveway, Robert allowed himself a small smile. "Oh, Mother," he said to the empty car, "you have no idea what's coming."

As the car disappeared into the night, the shadow of Robert's childhood home grew smaller in the rearview mirror. Ahead lay an uncertain future, filled with the promise of freedom and the potential for something far more sinister than Evelyn Langdon could ever imagine.

Chapter 2

The polished mahogany floor creaked softly under Robert's feet as he paced back and forth in his study. Each step echoed the restless thoughts swirling in his mind. The room, with its leather-bound books and antique globes, felt more like a gilded cage than a sanctuary.

Robert's gaze drifted to the large bay window, where raindrops raced down the glass, mirroring the turmoil within him. He sighed, running a hand through his perfectly coiffed hair.

"Another day, another battle," he muttered, his voice tinged with resignation.

His eyes landed on the crisp white envelope sitting on his desk. The sight of his mother's elegant handwriting made his stomach churn. With trembling fingers, he picked up the letter and began to read.

"Dearest Robert," he read aloud, mimicking Evelyn's authoritative tone. "I trust this letter finds you well and focused on your responsibilities."

He scoffed, shaking his head. "Focused on my responsibilities. As if I have a choice."

As he continued reading, his brow furrowed deeper with each line. The words seemed to leap off the page, each one a dagger to his already wounded spirit.

"I've taken the liberty of arranging a meeting with Senator Thompson next week. It's high time you considered a career in politics, as befitting your status and capabilities."

Robert's grip on the letter tightened, crumpling the expensive stationery. "My status and capabilities," he spat. "What about my desires, Mother?"

He continued pacing, his polished shoes clicking against the hardwood floor. The ticking of the antique grandfather clock in the corner seemed to grow louder, marking the seconds of his dwindling freedom.

"And regarding your personal life," he read on, his voice rising, "I've invited the Carmichael's daughter, Elizabeth, for dinner next month. She comes from an excellent family and would make a suitable match."

The letter fluttered to the floor as Robert's hands clenched into fists. He stared at his reflection in the window, barely recognizing the man looking back at him. Where was the charming, confident Robert Langdon the world knew? All he saw was a puppet, strings firmly in his mother's grasp.

"A suitable match," he whispered, his breath fogging the glass. "As if love and compatibility mean nothing."

He turned away from the window, his eyes landing on a framed photo of himself and Evelyn at his college graduation. Her smile was proud, but her hand on his shoulder seemed more possessive than affectionate.

"When will it be enough, Mother?" he asked the silent room. "When will I be allowed to live my own life?"

The only answer was the steady ticking of the clock and the patter of rain against the window, a somber soundtrack to his internal struggle.

Robert ran a hand through his perfectly coiffed hair, disheveling it in a rare moment of disarray. "God, I can't breathe," he muttered, tugging at his silk tie. "It's like she's always here, always watching, always... controlling."

He paced the length of his study, expensive Italian loafers clicking against the hardwood floor. "The right school, the right career, the right woman," he mocked, his voice taking on a shrill tone reminiscent of Evelyn's. "As if I'm some sort of... of puppet to be manipulated!"

Robert's eyes darted to his phone, sitting innocuously on his mahogany desk. A wild, desperate idea began to form in his mind. "No," he whispered, shaking his head. "I couldn't possibly..."

But even as he spoke, his feet carried him to the desk. His manicured fingers trembled as he picked up the device. "This is madness," he muttered, unlocking the screen. "Pure madness."

Yet he found himself opening a private browser, his heart pounding as he typed in a search query that made his blood run cold: "hire hitman."

As the results loaded, Robert's breath caught in his throat. "What am I doing?" he whispered, his charming facade crumbling as the weight of his actions settled on his shoulders. But he didn't close the browser. Instead, his finger hovered over the screen, ready to dive into a world from which there might be no return.

Robert's finger trembled as he scrolled through the dark web profiles, each one more menacing than the last. His usually confident demeanor crumbled, replaced by a palpable nervousness that made his palms sweat.

"This is insane," he muttered, running a hand through his perfectly coiffed hair. "I'm actually considering... No, I can't..."

But his eyes were drawn to one profile in particular: John Blackwood. The description was sparse, but the reviews were glowing in a chilling way. Robert's heart raced as he clicked the contact button.

The phone rang twice before a gruff voice answered, "Yeah?"

Robert swallowed hard. "Is this... John Blackwood?"

"Depends who's asking," came the measured reply.

"I... I need help with a... a problem," Robert stammered, his usual eloquence deserting him. He loosened his tie, feeling as if it were choking him. "It's my mother. She's... controlling every aspect of my life. I can't take it anymore."

There was a long pause on the other end. Robert could hear his own rapid breathing in the silence.

"What exactly are you asking?" John's voice was low, dangerous.

Robert closed his eyes, took a deep breath, and whispered, "I need her... gone. Permanently."

The words hung in the air, heavy with implication. Robert's mind raced with a mix of horror at what he'd just said and a twisted sense of relief.

"You understand what you're asking?" John's tone was neutral, but there was an undercurrent of something that made Robert shiver.

"Yes," Robert replied, his voice barely audible. "I do."

John's silence on the other end of the line stretched on, the tension palpable even through the phone. When he finally spoke, his words were measured and cautious. "Look, I don't know you. And this... this isn't something to be taken lightly."

Robert's grip tightened on his phone, knuckles turning white. He could feel his opportunity slipping away. "Please," he said, his voice cracking. "I understand the gravity of the situation. I wouldn't have reached out if I wasn't desperate."

"Desperation makes people do stupid things," John replied, his tone hardening. "It's not my problem."

Robert's mind raced. He couldn't let this chance go. "I can pay," he blurted out, pacing his study. "Whatever you want. Name your price."

There was a sharp intake of breath on the other end. "Money isn't everything," John said, but Robert detected a hint of interest.

"Five hundred thousand," Robert said quickly. "Cash. And I'll provide all the information you need. Her schedule, security details, everything."

John's voice lowered to a near whisper. "You realize what you're getting into? There's no going back from this."

Robert closed his eyes, picturing his mother's disapproving face. "I know," he said softly. "But I can't live like this anymore. Please... will you help me?"

A heavy sigh crackled through the phone, and Robert's heart leapt into his throat. He held his breath, waiting.

"Alright," John said finally, his voice barely above a whisper. "I'll do it."

Robert's knees nearly buckled with relief. He sank into his leather armchair, a trembling hand running through his perfectly coiffed hair. "Thank you," he breathed, a glimmer of hope igniting in his chest for the first time in years.

"Don't thank me yet," John warned, his tone razor-sharp. "We need to set some ground rules."

Robert nodded vigorously, even though John couldn't see him. "Of course, anything you say."

"First and foremost," John began, "absolute secrecy. You breathe a word of this to anyone, and the deal's off. And trust me, you don't want me as an enemy."

A chill ran down Robert's spine at the implicit threat. "Understood," he said quietly. "I won't tell a soul."

"Second," John continued, "I'll need half the payment up front. Non-negotiable."

Robert's mind raced, already calculating how to move the funds without raising suspicion. "Not a problem," he assured John. "I can have it ready within 48 hours."

"Good," John replied. "And Robert?"

"Yes?"

"Are you absolutely sure about this? Because once we start, there's no turning back. The consequences... they'll be on your head."

Robert closed his eyes, picturing a life free from his mother's suffocating control. The thought both terrified and exhilarated him. "I'm sure," he said, his voice steadier than he felt. "Whatever the consequences, I'll face them."

"Your funeral," John muttered, then paused. "Figuratively speaking, of course."

Despite the gravity of the situation, Robert found himself letting out a nervous chuckle. "Right," he said. "So, what's our next step?"

Robert paced the length of his study, his fingers tapping an anxious rhythm against his thigh. The weight of his decision pressed down on him like a physical force, making each breath a conscious effort.

"The best time," he said, his voice barely above a whisper, "would be during her daily walk. She's religious about it, never misses a day."

John's voice crackled through the phone's speaker. "Location?"

Robert swallowed hard, his throat suddenly dry. "There's a secluded path through Oakwood Park. She always takes it, precisely at 7 AM."

"Creatures of habit make this job easier," John remarked, a hint of dark amusement in his tone.

Robert's stomach churned. "There's a bench about halfway through. It's... it's where she likes to rest."

"Perfect," John said. "Any security we need to worry about?"

Robert shook his head, forgetting for a moment that John couldn't see him. "No, she's stubbornly independent. Refuses any kind of protection."

"Sounds like you've thought this through," John observed.

"I..." Robert hesitated, guilt washing over him. "I suppose I have."

The air in the room seemed to thicken, pressing in on Robert from all sides. He could hear his own heartbeat, a rapid staccato in his ears. His hand trembled as he reached for the briefcase on his desk.

"I have the payment," he said, his voice barely audible.

"Good," John replied. "I'll be there in ten minutes."

Robert ended the call, his finger lingering on the screen. *What have I done?* he thought, a wave of panic threatening to overwhelm him. But it was too late to turn back now.

The knock on the door came precisely ten minutes later. Robert opened it, revealing John's imposing figure. Without a word, John stepped inside, his eyes scanning the room with practiced efficiency.

Robert gestured to the briefcase. "It's all there," he said, his voice cracking slightly.

John nodded, picking up the case. The weight of it seemed to emphasize the gravity of their transaction. For a moment, neither man spoke, the silence broken only by the ticking of the antique clock on the mantle.

"Remember," John said finally, his eyes locking with Robert's, "once this is done, there's no going back."

Robert nodded, a bead of sweat trickling down his temple. "I understand."

As John turned to leave, Robert felt a strange mix of relief and terror. Their fates were now irrevocably intertwined, bound by a dark secret that would forever change both their lives.

Robert watched John's retreating figure, his heart pounding in his chest. As the door clicked shut, he exhaled sharply, running a trembling hand through his perfectly coiffed hair.

"What have I done?" he muttered, his polished facade crumbling. The weight of his decision bore down on him, threatening to crush his carefully constructed world.

He stumbled to the window, yanking open the heavy curtains. Outside, John's dark silhouette moved swiftly across the manicured lawn, disappearing into the shadows of the night.

Robert's mind raced, a torrent of conflicting emotions washing over him. Relief, guilt, and a perverse sense of anticipation battled for dominance.

"She'll be gone," he whispered, his breath fogging the glass. "I'll finally be free."

But even as the words left his lips, doubt crept in. Would he ever truly be free? Or had he just traded one prison for another?

The distant sound of a car engine starting made him flinch. John was leaving, carrying with him the means to change Robert's life forever.

"There's no going back now," Robert said to his reflection, his usually confident voice wavering. "God help me, there's no going back."

As the taillights faded into the distance, Robert was left alone with the weight of his choice, the future stretching before him like a dark and uncertain road.

Chapter 3

The precinct buzzed with activity as Detective Sarah Mitchell strode through the doors, her sharp eyes darting from desk to desk. The familiar scent of stale coffee and musty case files filled her nostrils. She absently smoothed her blazer, her mind already racing through potential assignments.

"Mitchell!" Captain Thompson's gruff voice cut through the din. "My office, now."

Sarah's eyebrows raised a fraction. What now? she wondered, weaving through the maze of desks. She rapped twice on the captain's door before entering.

"Close it," Thompson said, not looking up from his paperwork.

Sarah complied, settling into the chair across from him. She studied his furrowed brow, the tightness in his jaw. Whatever this was about, it was serious.

"You've got a new case," Thompson began, finally meeting her gaze. "Evelyn Langdon, 42. Found dead in her home this morning."

Sarah's mind kicked into high gear, questions forming rapidly. "Cause of death?"

"Still determining. But it's definitely homicide."

Sarah nodded, her fingers itching to start taking notes. "Any suspects?"

Thompson's lips thinned. "That's your job to find out, Mitchell. I'm assigning this to you because it's high-profile. Langdon was well-connected. The brass wants our best on this."

A mixture of pride and trepidation swirled in Sarah's gut. "Understood, sir. I'll get right on it."

"Good," Thompson said, sliding a file across his desk. "Everything we know so far is in here. Keep me updated."

As Sarah reached for the file, she couldn't help but feel a spark of excitement beneath her professional demeanor. This was what she lived for – unraveling the threads of a complex case, bringing justice to those who deserved it. She stood, tucking the file under her arm.

"I won't let you down, Captain," she said, her voice steady and determined.

Thompson's expression softened slightly. "I know you won't, Mitchell. That's why you're on this case."

Sarah's fingers tightened around the file as she left Thompson's office, her mind already racing. She paused at her desk, the bustling precinct fading into background noise as she opened the folder and saw Evelyn Langdon's photo staring back at her.

A lump formed in Sarah's throat. The elegant silver hair, the poised expression – it reminded her so much of her own mother. Memories of loss threatened to surface, but Sarah pushed them down, her jaw clenching.

"You okay, Mitchell?" Officer Chen called from nearby.

Sarah blinked, composing herself. "Yeah, fine. New case," she replied, her voice steady despite the emotions churning inside.

As she gathered her belongings, Sarah's thoughts drifted. "I know what it's like," she murmured to Evelyn's photo, "to lose someone suddenly. I'll find who did this to you."

Grabbing her jacket, Sarah headed for the exit. "Heading to the scene," she called to Chen. "Text me if anything urgent comes up."

The drive to the suburbs was a blur of determination and preparation. Sarah rehearsed her approach, steeling herself for what she might find. As she pulled up to the tidy house cordoned off with police tape, a familiar mix of anticipation and dread settled in her stomach.

"Time to get to work," Sarah muttered, stepping out of her car. She took a deep breath, centering herself. Then, with purposeful strides, she approached the house where Evelyn Langdon's life had come to a violent end.

Sarah ducked under the yellow police tape, her eyes immediately scanning the pristine suburban lawn. The contrast between the manicured hedges and the grim reality within sent a chill down her spine.

As she entered the house, the coppery scent of blood hit her nostrils. The living room was a tableau of violence frozen in time. Shattered glass crunched under her feet, and overturned furniture spoke of a fierce struggle.

"Detective Mitchell," a voice called. It was Dr. Ramirez, the lead forensic analyst, crouched near a dark stain on the beige carpet. "Victim's blood. Spatter pattern suggests multiple blows."

Sarah nodded, her keen eyes taking in every detail. "Time of death?"

"Preliminary estimate, between 9 and 11 PM last night," Ramirez replied, carefully bagging a blood-stained object.

Sarah's gaze fell on a collection of family photos on the mantle. Evelyn's smiling face stared back at her, surrounded by loved ones. A pang of empathy stabbed through Sarah's professional detachment.

Shaking it off, she turned to the nearest uniformed officer. "Any witnesses?"

"Neighbors heard a commotion, but no one saw anything definitive," he reported. "They're pretty shaken up."

Sarah's brow furrowed. "I'll need to talk to them. Where are they now?"

"Gathered at the house next door. But fair warning, they're not exactly forthcoming."

Sarah sighed inwardly. "Of course not. When are they ever?" She squared her shoulders, preparing for the challenge ahead. "Time to see what they're not saying."

As she approached the neighbor's house, Sarah observed the cluster of people on the porch, their hushed conversations falling silent at her approach. She put on her most disarming smile, though her eyes remained sharp and focused.

"Good afternoon," she began, her tone gentle but authoritative. "I'm Detective Sarah Mitchell. I know this is a difficult time, but I need to ask you all a few questions about last night."

The neighbors exchanged uneasy glances. An older woman stepped forward, wringing her hands. "We've already told the other officers everything we know."

Sarah nodded sympathetically. "I understand, ma'am. But sometimes, even the smallest detail can make a big difference. You never know what might help us catch whoever did this to your neighbor."

She paused, letting her words sink in. Then, with a slight tilt of her head, Sarah added, "Evelyn deserves justice, doesn't she?"

The tension in the group visibly eased, and Sarah suppressed a small smile. She had found her opening. Now, it was time to unravel the truth, one reluctant witness at a time.

Sarah's frustration mounted as she moved from one neighbor to the next. Despite her best efforts, their responses remained vague and evasive. She pinched the bridge of her nose, feeling a headache coming on.

"I understand you're scared," she said to a middle-aged man who kept glancing nervously over his shoulder. "But anything you can tell me—"

"Look," he interrupted, lowering his voice. "We all liked Evelyn, but she kept to herself. That's how it is around here. We mind our own business."

Sarah's eyes narrowed. There was something in his tone, a hint of... what? Fear? Guilt? She couldn't quite place it, but her instincts were screaming that there was more to uncover.

As she walked away, Sarah's mind raced. She needed a new approach. Suddenly, an idea struck her. She pulled out her phone and dialed a number.

"Dr. Shaw's office," a crisp voice answered.

"This is Detective Sarah Mitchell. I need to speak with Dr. Elizabeth Shaw urgently."

There was a pause. "I'm sorry, Detective, but Dr. Shaw's schedule is fully booked for the next two weeks."

Sarah gritted her teeth. "This is about the Langdon murder case. Please, it's crucial that I speak with her."

Another pause. "Hold on, please."

As she waited, Sarah's gaze drifted back to Evelyn's house. The elegant facade seemed to mock her, hiding its secrets. She thought of Evelyn, of the life cut short, and felt a renewed surge of determination.

"Detective Mitchell?" Dr. Shaw's voice came through the line, warm but professional. "I understand you need my assistance."

Sarah exhaled, relief flooding through her. "Dr. Shaw, thank you for taking my call. I'm investigating Evelyn Langdon's murder, and I could use your expertise. The witnesses are... challenging."

"Ah, the psychology of silence," Dr. Shaw mused. "Fascinating, isn't it? When can we meet?"

Sarah's shoulders relaxed slightly as she stepped into Dr. Shaw's office. The room exuded calm, with its muted earth tones and soft lighting.

Dr. Shaw rose from behind her desk, extending a hand. "Detective Mitchell, it's a pleasure to meet you in person."

Sarah shook her hand firmly. "Thank you for seeing me on such short notice, Dr. Shaw."

"Please, have a seat," Dr. Shaw gestured to a comfortable armchair. "Now, tell me about the witnesses you're struggling with."

Sarah leaned forward, her brow furrowed. "They're tight-lipped, almost... scared. But of what, I'm not sure."

Dr. Shaw nodded thoughtfully. "Fear is a powerful motivator, Detective. It can manifest in many ways, including silence."

"But what could they be afraid of?" Sarah mused, more to herself than to Dr. Shaw.

"Perhaps it's not what, but who," Dr. Shaw suggested. "In cases like these, the perpetrator often has a connection to the community. Someone respected, or feared."

Sarah's eyes widened slightly. She hadn't considered that angle. "That would explain the resistance I'm encountering."

Dr. Shaw leaned back in her chair. "Consider the victim's social circle. Who held power or influence? Look for subtle patterns of control or manipulation."

As Dr. Shaw spoke, Sarah felt a renewed sense of purpose. Her mind raced, connecting dots she hadn't seen before.

After leaving Dr. Shaw's office, Sarah drove straight back to the crime scene. The suburban street was quiet now, the initial flurry of police activity long gone. She parked her car and sat for a moment, Dr. Shaw's words echoing in her mind.

Taking a deep breath, she stepped out and approached Evelyn's house. The yellow crime scene tape fluttered in the breeze, a stark reminder of the tragedy that had unfolded here.

Sarah ducked under the tape and entered the house. The air inside was still, heavy with the lingering scent of forensic chemicals. She moved methodically through each room, her trained eyes scrutinizing every surface, every shadow.

In the living room, she paused. Something about the bookshelf caught her attention. She couldn't put her finger on it, but something seemed... off. Sarah stepped closer, running her fingers along the spines of the books. Her breath caught as she felt a slight give in one of the shelves.

Sarah's heart raced as she carefully pulled the shelf forward, revealing a hidden compartment behind it. Her eyes widened as she spotted a faint, reddish-brown smudge on the edge of the opening. A bloody handprint.

"Gotcha," she whispered, her voice barely audible in the stillness of the room.

With trembling hands, Sarah reached for her phone, snapping several photos of the discovery. The gravity of the find sent a shiver down her spine. This could be the breakthrough they'd been waiting for.

As she stared at the handprint, her mind whirred with possibilities. Who had left it there? Was it the killer's? Or perhaps Evelyn's, as she fought for her life?

Sarah took a deep breath, steadying herself. She needed her team. Pulling out her phone once more, she dialed Kevin's number.

"Johnson," came the eager voice on the other end.

"Kevin, it's Mitchell. I need you and Carter at the Langdon house ASAP. We've got something."

"On it, Detective," Kevin replied, his excitement palpable even through the phone. "We'll be there in ten."

As she waited, Sarah paced the room, her eyes continually drawn back to the hidden compartment. The anticipation was almost unbearable.

When Kevin and Linda arrived, Sarah ushered them inside, her usual stoic demeanor cracking with barely contained excitement.

"What've we got, Detective?" Kevin asked, his eyes bright with curiosity.

Sarah led them to the bookshelf. "Take a look," she said, gesturing to the hidden compartment.

Linda gasped. "Is that...?"

"A bloody handprint," Sarah confirmed. "Hidden away where no one would think to look."

Kevin leaned in closer, his brow furrowed in concentration. "This is huge, isn't it?"

Sarah nodded, a small smile playing at the corners of her mouth. "It could be the key to cracking this case wide open."

Sarah's piercing eyes scanned the room, taking in the evidence boards and scattered case files. Her team huddled around the conference table, their faces a mix of determination and exhaustion.

"Alright, let's connect the dots," Sarah said, her voice crisp and focused. "What do we know?"

Kevin, the eager rookie, jumped in. "We've got the hidden handprint, which suggests the killer might have known the house well enough to find that compartment."

Linda, the social worker, nodded. "And from the witnesses, we know Evelyn was last seen arguing with someone the day before her murder. A man, middle-aged, well-dressed."

Sarah paced, her mind racing. "Good. What else?"

"The autopsy report," Kevin added, rifling through papers. "Cause of death was strangulation, but there were defensive wounds on her hands."

Sarah paused, a memory flickering. "Evelyn's son, Robert. He had scratches on his face when we interviewed him. Said it was from gardening."

Linda's eyes widened. "You think he could be involved?"

"It's a possibility we can't ignore," Sarah replied, her tone measured. She turned to the evidence board, pinning up a photo of Robert. "He stood to inherit everything, and we know he and Evelyn had a strained relationship."

As she stepped back, Sarah felt a familiar tightness in her chest. The case was hitting close to home, reminding her of her own loss. She pushed the feeling aside, focusing on the task at hand.

"We're getting closer," she murmured, more to herself than the others. "I can feel it."

Suddenly, Kevin's phone buzzed. He answered, his expression shifting from curiosity to shock.

"Detective," he said, hanging up. "You're not going to believe this. They found another body."

Sarah's head snapped up, her eyes locking with Kevin's. "Where?"

"Three blocks from the Langdon house. Same M.O."

The room fell silent as the implications sank in. Sarah's mind raced with possibilities. Was this a copycat? Or had they been wrong about the killer's motives all along?

"Gear up," she ordered, grabbing her jacket. "We've got a new crime scene to process."

As they rushed out, Sarah couldn't shake the feeling that this case was about to take a dark and unexpected turn. Whatever lay ahead, she was determined to see it through, no matter the cost.

Chapter 4

Sarah Mitchell stood before the polished wooden door, her hand hovering over the brass nameplate that read "Dr. Elizabeth Shaw, Criminal Psychologist." A faint whiff of lemon-scented cleaner tickled her nose as she inhaled deeply, steeling herself.

This is ridiculous, she thought. *I don't need a shrink to do my job.* But as she exhaled, Sarah felt a flicker of curiosity. Maybe this Dr. Shaw could offer a fresh perspective on the case that had been keeping her up at night.

With a resigned sigh, Sarah pushed open the door and stepped into a warmly lit waiting room. Soft classical music drifted from hidden speakers, and the walls were adorned with soothing abstract paintings. Despite herself, Sarah felt some of the tension leave her shoulders.

"Detective Mitchell?" A gentle voice drew Sarah's attention to a woman emerging from an inner office. Dr. Elizabeth Shaw moved with quiet grace, her silver-streaked hair framing a face etched with laugh lines. "I'm Dr. Shaw. It's a pleasure to meet you."

As they shook hands, Sarah was struck by the warmth in Dr. Shaw's eyes. It was disarming, almost maternal, and Sarah felt her skepticism wavering.

"Thank you for seeing me on such short notice, Dr. Shaw," Sarah said, her tone clipped and professional.

Dr. Shaw smiled, gesturing towards her office. "Of course. Please, come in and make yourself comfortable."

Sarah followed her into a cozy room lined with bookshelves. She perched on the edge of a plush armchair, her back ramrod straight as she surveyed her surroundings. *No couch*, she noted with a hint of amusement. *At least she's not a cliché*.

"Can I offer you some tea?" Dr. Shaw asked, settling into her own chair.

"No, thank you," Sarah replied, her fingers drumming against her thigh. "I appreciate you taking the time to consult on this case."

Dr. Shaw leaned forward slightly, her expression open and engaged. "I'm always eager to assist law enforcement in any way I can. Why don't you tell me a bit about what brings you here today?"

As Sarah began to speak, she found herself relaxing incrementally. There was something about Dr. Shaw's presence – a blend of warmth and professionalism – that put her at ease. For the first time in days, Sarah felt a glimmer of hope that she might finally make some headway on this baffling case.

Sarah took a deep breath, organizing her thoughts before diving into the details. "We're dealing with a particularly gruesome murder. A young woman, Emily Thompson, was found dead in her apartment three days ago. The cause of death was strangulation, but..." She paused, her brow furrowing. "There were... unusual elements to the crime scene."

Dr. Shaw nodded encouragingly. "Go on, Detective Mitchell. What struck you as unusual?"

"The body was posed," Sarah continued, her voice tightening. "Arranged like a piece of art. And there were symbols drawn on the walls in the victim's blood. We haven't been able to decipher their meaning yet."

As she spoke, Sarah couldn't help but notice Dr. Shaw's intense focus. The psychologist's eyes never left her face, and Sarah found herself wondering what insights those keen eyes might be gleaning.

"That does sound quite complex," Dr. Shaw mused. "Have you identified any suspects so far?"

Sarah shook her head, frustration evident in her tense shoulders. "Nothing concrete. That's partly why I'm here. We need a fresh perspective, someone who can help us understand the killer's mindset."

Dr. Shaw leaned back in her chair, her fingers steepled beneath her chin. "I see. Tell me, Detective, what was your initial impression when you first entered the crime scene?"

The question caught Sarah off guard. She blinked, momentarily thrown by the directness of the inquiry. "I... well, it was unlike anything I'd seen before. The level of meticulous care taken with the body was... unsettling."

"Interesting," Dr. Shaw murmured. "And the symbols – you mentioned they were drawn in blood. Were they uniform in size and shape, or did they vary?"

Sarah's eyes widened slightly. It wasn't a detail she'd expected the psychologist to hone in on. "They varied," she replied, her mind racing back to the scene. "Some were larger, more elaborate. Others were smaller, almost like footnotes."

As Dr. Shaw continued to ask probing questions, Sarah found herself impressed by the psychologist's ability to zero in on seemingly innocuous details. With each response, she felt as though she were seeing the crime scene through fresh eyes.

Dr. Shaw nodded thoughtfully, her eyes gleaming with insight. "Based on what you've shared, Detective Mitchell, I believe we're dealing with someone who craves attention and recognition. The varying sizes of the symbols suggest a hierarchy of importance to the killer – a sort of coded message they're desperate for us to decipher."

Sarah leaned forward, her skepticism giving way to intrigue. "You can tell that just from the symbol sizes?"

"It's not just the symbols," Dr. Shaw explained, her tone warm but authoritative. "It's the overall presentation. The meticulous care taken with the body, the elaborate staging – this isn't just a crime, it's a performance. Our killer wants an audience."

Sarah felt a small shiver run down her spine. She'd been so focused on the physical evidence, she'd nearly missed the psychological implications. "That... actually makes a lot of sense," she admitted, her respect for Dr. Shaw growing.

Dr. Shaw smiled gently. "Criminal psychology isn't about mind-reading, Detective. It's about understanding patterns of behavior and motivation. In this case, I'd wager our perpetrator feels undervalued or overlooked in their daily life. This crime is their way of demanding attention."

Sarah nodded, her mind racing with new possibilities. She'd come here out of obligation, but now she found herself genuinely eager to hear more. "Do you think they'll strike again?" she asked, leaning forward in her chair.

"That depends," Dr. Shaw replied, her expression thoughtful. "If they don't receive the recognition they're seeking, it's certainly possible. But your investigation itself might satisfy that need for attention, at least temporarily."

As Dr. Shaw continued to share her insights, Sarah found herself mentally reassessing her initial reservations about consulting a psychologist. The doctor's ability to extract meaning from the tiniest details was impressive, to say the least.

Maybe, Sarah thought, there was more to this psychology stuff than she'd given credit for.

Dr. Shaw leaned back in her chair, her eyes focused intently on Sarah. "Based on the details you've shared, Detective Mitchell, I believe we're dealing with someone who craves recognition and control. The meticulous nature of the crime scene suggests a person who's highly organized, possibly even obsessive-compulsive in their daily life."

Sarah's brow furrowed as she processed this information. "So, we might be looking for someone in a position of little authority, but who believes they deserve more?"

"Precisely," Dr. Shaw nodded, a hint of approval in her voice. "The killer likely feels underappreciated in their professional or personal life.

The murder could be their way of asserting dominance and proving their intelligence."

Sarah's mind raced, connecting dots she hadn't seen before. "What about the victim's background? Could that play into the killer's motives?"

Dr. Shaw's eyes lit up at the question. "Absolutely. The choice of victim is rarely random in cases like these. Was there anything notable about their social status or career?"

Sarah pulled out her notebook, flipping through pages of scribbled notes. "The victim was a successful business owner, well-liked in the community. Could that be significant?"

"Indeed," Dr. Shaw replied, leaning forward. "The killer might have chosen this victim as a symbol of the success they feel they've been denied. It's a way of lashing out at a society they believe has wronged them."

Sarah's pen moved rapidly across the page, capturing every word. She couldn't shake the feeling that they were on the verge of a breakthrough. "So, we should be looking for someone who might have had professional dealings with the victim? Someone who felt slighted or overlooked?"

Dr. Shaw nodded, her expression both grave and encouraging. "That would be a good place to start, Detective. Pay close attention to individuals who might have been passed over for promotions or business opportunities. Your killer is likely someone who believes they're far more capable than others give them credit for."

As the implications of Dr. Shaw's analysis sank in, Sarah felt a renewed sense of purpose. She had come here skeptical, but now she saw the value of this psychological perspective. It was like gaining a new set of eyes to view the evidence through.

Sarah set her notebook down, meeting Dr. Shaw's gaze with newfound respect. "You know, when I first came here, I wasn't sure how much this would help. But the way you've broken down the killer's possible motivations... it's given me a whole new perspective."

Dr. Shaw's eyes crinkled with warmth. "I'm glad to hear that, Detective Mitchell. It's not always easy to see the human element behind these horrific acts, but understanding it is crucial to solving them."

"You're right," Sarah nodded, a rueful smile playing on her lips. "I've spent so long focusing on the physical evidence, sometimes I forget there's a person—twisted as they may be—behind it all."

Dr. Shaw leaned back in her chair, her posture relaxing. "It's a common pitfall in law enforcement. We're all working towards the same goal—justice—but from different angles. Your forensic expertise combined with psychological profiling can be a powerful tool."

Sarah felt a sudden kinship with the older woman. Despite their different approaches, they shared a deep-seated desire to uncover the truth and bring closure to victims' families.

"I can't thank you enough for your insights, Dr. Shaw," Sarah said, standing up and extending her hand. "You've given me a lot to think about, and some solid leads to pursue."

Dr. Shaw stood as well, grasping Sarah's hand firmly. "It's been my pleasure, Detective. Remember, the mind is a complex landscape. Don't be afraid to reach out if you need further guidance navigating it."

As they shook hands, Sarah felt a surge of gratitude and determination. She had entered this office full of doubt, but was leaving with a renewed sense of purpose and a valuable ally in her quest for justice.

Dr. Shaw's eyes sparkled with understanding as she released Sarah's hand. "Before you go, Detective Mitchell, I want you to remember something crucial," she said, her voice warm but firm. "Trust your instincts. They've brought you this far for a reason."

Sarah hesitated, her brow furrowing slightly. "Even when they seem to contradict the evidence?"

Dr. Shaw nodded, a knowing smile playing on her lips. "Especially then. Your instincts are honed by years of experience. They're picking up on subtle cues your conscious mind might miss." She paused, tapping her chin thoughtfully. "Think of them as whispers from your subconscious. They're worth listening to."

The detective felt a flicker of validation. How many times had she second-guessed herself, pushing aside hunches in favor of cold, hard facts?

"I'll keep that in mind," Sarah replied, her voice steady but her mind racing with possibilities.

As she gathered her notes, Dr. Shaw added, "And remember, my door is always open. This case sounds complex - don't hesitate to reach out if you need a sounding board."

Sarah nodded gratefully, feeling a unexpected warmth bloom in her chest. It had been a long time since she'd allowed herself to rely on anyone else.

Stepping out of Dr. Shaw's office, Sarah took a deep breath. The late afternoon sun slanted through the windows, casting long shadows across the hallway. She felt lighter somehow, as if the weight of the investigation had been redistributed.

'Time to get back to work,' she thought, a newfound energy coursing through her veins. As she strode towards the elevator, her mind was already piecing together the puzzle, viewing the evidence through a fresh lens.

For the first time in weeks, Sarah felt a glimmer of hope. She wasn't just chasing a killer anymore - she was unraveling a complex human story. And with Dr. Shaw's insights as her guide, she was more determined than ever to write its final chapter.

Chapter 5

The Langdon family estate loomed before Robert as he pulled into the circular driveway, its manicured hedges and gleaming windows a testament to his mother's exacting standards. He adjusted his silk tie, took a deep breath, and stepped out of his Mercedes.

"Another Sunday, another inquisition," he muttered, striding towards the imposing front door.

As he raised his hand to knock, the door swung open to reveal Evelyn Langdon, her silver hair immaculate and her posture ramrod straight.

"You're late, Robert," she said, her lips pursed in disapproval.

Robert checked his watch. "By two minutes, Mother. I'm sure the roast won't have time to get cold."

Evelyn's eyes narrowed, but she stepped aside to let him enter. The familiar scent of lemon polish and old money enveloped him as he walked into the foyer.

"I read about your latest acquisition in the Wall Street Journal," Evelyn said, leading him towards the dining room. "Impressive, I suppose, though I would have negotiated a better deal."

Robert's jaw clenched. Even his multi-million dollar business deals weren't good enough for her. He forced a smile. "Well, we can't all be as shrewd as you, Mother."

As they sat down to dinner, Robert's mind wandered to his recent achievements: the new tech startup he'd funded, the charity gala he'd organized, the glowing profile in Forbes. Yet none of it seemed to matter in this room, under his mother's critical gaze.

"How's the Hartley merger coming along?" Evelyn asked, cutting into her roast with surgical precision.

Robert suppressed a sigh. "It's progressing. These things take time."

"Time is money, Robert. You should know that by now."

He nodded, feeling the familiar weight of her expectations pressing down on him. As he mechanically ate his dinner, he couldn't help but wonder: when would it ever be enough? When would he finally feel like he'd made her proud?

The sound of tires on gravel caught his attention, and he glanced out the window to see a beat-up pickup truck pull into the driveway. A scruffy-looking man in worn jeans and a leather jacket stepped out, his intense gaze sweeping over the property.

"Who on earth is that?" Evelyn asked, her voice dripping with disdain.

Robert shrugged, an inexplicable feeling of unease settling in his stomach. "Probably just lost. I'm sure he'll be on his way soon."

As he turned back to his meal, Robert couldn't shake the feeling that something was about to change. Little did he know, the arrival of John Blackwood would set in motion a chain of events that would shatter the carefully constructed facade of the Langdon family forever.

Evelyn's silverware clinked against her plate as she set it down, her posture stiffening. "I'll have Thomas see to it," she said, referring to their longtime butler.

But before she could summon him, Robert stood. "No, I'll handle it." He welcomed the excuse to escape the suffocating dining room.

As he made his way to the front door, Evelyn's voice drifted after him. "Don't dawdle, Robert. We have matters to discuss."

Outside, the cool evening air offered momentary relief. Robert approached the stranger, who leaned against his truck, arms crossed.

"Can I help you?" Robert asked, forcing a polite smile.

The man's piercing gaze met his. "John Blackwood. I'm here about the... job."

Robert's heart skipped a beat. This was the man he'd contacted, the one who could solve all his problems. He glanced back at the house, lowering his voice. "Not here. Meet me at the boathouse in an hour."

John nodded, his expression unreadable. As he climbed back into his truck, Robert couldn't help but wonder what dark paths this man had walked to end up here, in this moment.

Returning inside, Robert found Evelyn waiting in the hallway, her arms crossed. "Well? Who was it?"

"Just someone looking for directions," he lied smoothly. "I sent him on his way."

Evelyn's eyes narrowed, searching his face. "Very well. Now, about the Hartley merger..."

As she launched into a lecture on corporate strategy, Robert's mind drifted. He thought of his mother's relentless drive, the way she'd molded him since childhood. But for the first time, he also saw the toll it had taken on her – the fine lines etched around her eyes, the tension in her shoulders.

For a fleeting moment, he almost felt sorry for her. Almost.

Robert forced himself to focus on his mother's words, nodding at appropriate intervals as she dissected the intricacies of the Hartley merger. His charm kicked in automatically, a defense mechanism honed over years of navigating Evelyn's expectations.

"You're absolutely right, Mother," he interjected smoothly, flashing his trademark smile. "I'll make sure to emphasize those points in tomorrow's meeting."

Evelyn paused, a hint of approval flickering across her face. "Good. I expect nothing less than perfection, Robert. You know how crucial this deal is for the company."

As she spoke, Robert felt the familiar weight of her expectations settle on his shoulders. He rolled them discreetly, trying to ease the tension. "Of course, Mother. I won't let you down."

"See that you don't," Evelyn replied, her tone softening slightly. She reached out, adjusting his tie with practiced precision. "You have so much potential, darling. I just want to see you reach it."

Robert swallowed hard, conflicting emotions churning inside him. Part of him longed for her approval, while another part seethed with resentment. He forced another smile, "I know, Mother. Thank you for always pushing me to be my best."

As Evelyn turned to leave, Robert caught a glimpse of vulnerability in her eyes – a fleeting moment of doubt, perhaps? – before her mask of elegance slipped back into place. He watched her go, his mind racing.

"I need some air," he muttered to himself, heading for the back door. As he stepped outside, his thoughts turned to John Blackwood and their impending meeting. Was he really going to go through with this? The weight of his decision pressed down on him, threatening to suffocate him with each passing second.

The crisp evening air hit Robert's face as he stepped onto the terrace, the scent of jasmine from the garden below wafting up to greet him. He inhaled deeply, trying to calm his racing thoughts. The distant sound of traffic hummed in the background, a reminder of the world beyond his gilded cage.

"Rough night?" a gravelly voice asked from the shadows.

Robert started, his hand instinctively reaching for his chest. "Christ, John. You nearly gave me a heart attack."

John Blackwood emerged from the darkness, a cigarette dangling from his lips. The orange glow illuminated his rugged features for a moment before fading. "Figured you might need some company after that little chat with the Ice Queen."

Robert's jaw clenched. "She means well," he said, the words sounding hollow even to his own ears.

John snorted, taking a long drag. "Yeah, and I'm the Pope." He fixed Robert with an intense stare. "You don't have to pretend with me, Langdon. I've seen how she treats you."

The tension in Robert's shoulders eased slightly. There was something oddly comforting about John's bluntness. "It's... complicated," he admitted, leaning against the railing.

"Always is with family," John replied, his tone softer now. He offered Robert the cigarette, which he declined with a wave.

"How much did you hear?" Robert asked, curiosity getting the better of him.

John shrugged. "Enough to know you're caught between a rock and a hard place." He paused, considering his next words carefully. "Look, I'm not one for giving advice, but sometimes you gotta choose your own path, even if it pisses off the people you love."

Robert laughed bitterly. "Easier said than done when your mother holds the purse strings to your entire life."

"There are always options," John said cryptically, stubbing out his cigarette. "You just gotta be willing to take risks."

As they stood in companionable silence, Robert found himself studying John's profile. What kind of risks had this man taken in his life? And more importantly, what kind of risks was Robert willing to take to break free from his mother's suffocating expectations?

The moment was shattered by Evelyn's voice calling from inside. "Robert? Where are you? The Hendersons have arrived."

Robert straightened, adjusting his tie once more. He shot John a rueful smile. "Duty calls."

As he turned to go, John's hand on his arm stopped him. "Remember what I said, Langdon. There's always a choice."

Robert nodded, a mix of gratitude and unease swirling in his stomach as he headed back inside to face the music.

Robert's mind raced as he navigated the crowded living room, his practiced smile barely masking the turmoil within. John's words echoed in his head, a dangerous whisper of possibility.

"There you are, darling," Evelyn cooed, her manicured nails digging into his arm. "The Hendersons were just asking about your latest acquisition."

Robert launched into his rehearsed spiel, but his thoughts were elsewhere. Each passing minute felt like a noose tightening around his neck. He excused himself, retreating to his father's old study.

Surrounded by leather-bound books and the lingering scent of cigars, Robert's resolve crumbled. He pulled out his phone, fingers hovering over John's number.

"This is insane," he muttered, running a hand through his hair.

But the thought of another decade under his mother's thumb, of suffocating beneath the weight of her expectations... It was too much.

With trembling hands, he typed: "We need to talk. Privately."

John's reply came swiftly: "Tomorrow. Noon. The old boathouse."

Robert stared at the screen, a mix of dread and exhilaration coursing through him. There was no going back now.

As he rejoined the party, Evelyn's gaze locked onto him. "Everything alright, dear?"

Robert smiled, a newfound lightness in his step. "Never better, Mother. Never better."

Little did she know, her son had just taken the first step towards her demise.

Robert's newfound resolve carried him through the rest of the evening, his practiced charm on full display as he navigated the crowd. As the last guest departed, Evelyn approached him, her eyes narrowing with suspicion.

"You seem... different tonight, Robert," she mused, studying his face. "More relaxed. I hope you're not letting your standards slip."

Robert chuckled, the sound hollow to his own ears. "Just enjoying the evening, Mother. Nothing to worry about."

As Evelyn retired to her room, Robert found himself drawn to the kitchen, where he poured a generous whiskey. The amber liquid sloshed in his glass as he made his way to the patio, the cool night air a welcome respite.

Meanwhile, across town, John Blackwood hunched over a battered laptop in his dimly lit apartment. His fingers flew across the keyboard, pulling up information on the Langdon family. A slow smile spread across his face as he pieced together the puzzle of Robert's request.

"Well, well," he muttered, leaning back in his chair. "Looks like the golden boy's got a dark side after all."

The next morning, Robert woke early, his stomach churning with anticipation. He dressed casually, hoping to avoid his mother's scrutiny. As he descended the stairs, Evelyn's voice rang out from the dining room.

"Robert, dear, join me for breakfast. We need to discuss the charity gala next month."

He gritted his teeth, forcing a smile as he entered the room. "Of course, Mother. But I'm afraid I have a meeting at noon. Perhaps we could chat this evening?"

Evelyn's lips pursed, but she nodded. "Very well. Don't be late for dinner."

As the clock struck twelve, Robert found himself standing before the weathered boathouse. John emerged from the shadows, his eyes darting around before settling on Robert.

"You sure about this?" John asked, his voice low and gravelly.

Robert swallowed hard, nodding. "I've never been more certain of anything in my life."

Robert's heart raced as he stood face-to-face with John, the weight of his decision pressing down on him like a physical force. He could feel beads of sweat forming on his brow, and he resisted the urge to wipe them away, not wanting to show any sign of weakness.

"It's just..." Robert hesitated, his voice barely above a whisper. "Once we do this, there's no going back."

John's eyes narrowed, studying Robert's face intently. "Having second thoughts, rich boy?"

Robert straightened his posture, squaring his shoulders. "No. It's the only way."

As they spoke, Robert's mind flashed back to countless dinner parties and charity events where his mother's disapproving gaze had followed his every move. He could almost hear her voice, sharp and critical: "Stand up straight, Robert. A Langdon always presents themselves with dignity."

John's rough chuckle snapped Robert back to the present. "Alright then. Let's talk details."

They moved deeper into the shadows of the boathouse, the musty scent of damp wood filling Robert's nostrils. As John laid out the plan in hushed tones, Robert felt a strange mix of relief and terror washing over him.

"You understand what this means, don't you?" John asked, his voice carrying a hint of challenge. "Once it's done, your life changes forever."

Robert nodded, his throat dry. "I know. But living under her thumb... it's not really living at all."

As he spoke the words aloud, Robert felt a sudden, overwhelming sense of guilt. He thought of his mother's rare moments of warmth, the pride in her eyes when he'd graduated from Harvard. But then the memory shifted, morphing into the disappointment that had followed when he'd chosen a different career path than she'd planned.

"You're sure you can handle this?" John pressed, interrupting Robert's thoughts.

Robert met John's gaze, his voice steady despite the turmoil inside. "I have to. It's the only way I'll ever be free."

Chapter 6

Sarah Mitchell strode into the police station, her jaw set with determination. The familiar scent of coffee and stale donuts hung in the air, but she barely noticed as she made her way to her desk. Her piercing eyes scanned the room, taking in every detail as if searching for hidden clues.

"Morning, Detective Mitchell," Officer Johnson called out. "Ready to crack this case wide open?"

Sarah offered a tight smile. "One step at a time, Johnson. But I'm hoping today brings us closer."

She settled into her chair, pulling the case files toward her. The weight of the folders felt heavier than usual, laden with the responsibility of bringing a killer to justice. Sarah's fingers traced the edge of a photograph of Evelyn's smiling face stared back at her, unaware of the fate that awaited her.

As she delved into the witness statements, Sarah's brow furrowed. Something wasn't adding up. She muttered to herself, "Why are they all so... hesitant?"

"Talking to yourself again, Mitchell?" Detective Garcia chuckled as he passed by her desk.

Sarah looked up, her expression serious. "Garcia, have you noticed anything odd about these witness statements?"

He shrugged. "Other than the fact that nobody seems to want to talk? Not really."

Sarah nodded, her suspicions confirmed. "Exactly. It's like they're all holding something back. But why?"

She turned back to the files, her mind racing. Could the witnesses be afraid? Or was there something more sinister at play? Sarah's instincts, honed by years on the force, told her she was missing a crucial piece of the puzzle.

As she pored over the statements again, Sarah couldn't shake the feeling that time was running out. She thought to herself, "I need to figure out what's making these witnesses clam up. And fast."

Her eyes landed on a particular statement, and she leaned in closer, her heart rate quickening. "This could be it," she whispered, a glimmer of hope sparking in her eyes.

Sarah's eyes narrowed as she read the name on the witness statement: Mrs. Jenkins. She stood up, grabbing her notebook and heading for the door. The cool autumn air hit her face as she stepped outside, her mind already formulating a strategy.

Mrs. Jenkins' house was a quaint little bungalow, its well-tended garden a stark contrast to the tension Sarah felt as she approached the front door. She took a deep breath, reminding herself to tread carefully. This witness could be the key to unlocking the whole case.

As the door creaked open, Sarah's keen eyes immediately took in every detail. Mrs. Jenkins, a petite woman in her seventies, stood before her, anxiety etched across her face.

"Mrs. Jenkins?" Sarah asked, her voice deliberately soft. "I'm Detective Sarah Mitchell. I was hoping we could talk about what you saw the night of Ms. Langdon's murder."

Mrs. Jenkins' fingers tightened on the doorknob. "I... I don't know if I should say anything more."

Sarah nodded empathetically. "I understand you're afraid, Mrs. Jenkins. May I come in? I promise, I'm here to help."

After a moment's hesitation, Mrs. Jenkins stepped aside. Sarah entered, noting the immaculate living room and the faint scent of lavender in the air.

"Would you like some tea?" Mrs. Jenkins offered, her voice wavering slightly.

"That would be lovely, thank you," Sarah replied, recognizing the offer as a chance for Mrs. Jenkins to gather her thoughts.

As they settled into floral-patterned armchairs, steaming cups in hand, Sarah leaned forward slightly. "Mrs. Jenkins, can you tell me about the figure you saw that night?"

Mrs. Jenkins' hands trembled, causing her teacup to clink against its saucer. "It was dark, you see. I couldn't make out much."

"That's okay," Sarah encouraged gently. "Even the smallest detail could be important. What made the figure suspicious to you?"

Sarah's eyes narrowed as she approached the imposing oak door of Mr. Thompson's office. She'd spent the better part of the afternoon trying to secure this meeting, and she wasn't about to let her opportunity slip away. Taking a deep breath, she rapped her knuckles against the polished wood.

"Come in," a gruff voice called from within.

Sarah stepped into the dimly lit room, her gaze immediately drawn to the man behind the desk. Mr. Thompson, a portly gentleman in his mid-fifties, regarded her with clear disdain.

"Mr. Thompson, I appreciate you agreeing to meet with me," Sarah began, her tone professional yet warm.

He grunted, leaning back in his chair. "I've got five minutes, Detective. Make it quick."

Sarah's mind raced, searching for the right approach. She decided on directness. "I understand you and Evelyn Langdon had a... complicated working relationship."

Mr. Thompson's face tightened. "That's putting it mildly. Look, I've already told the police everything I know."

"I'm sure you have," Sarah replied, taking a seat across from him. "But sometimes, small details can make a big difference. Is there anything you might have remembered since then?"

He hesitated, and Sarah caught a flicker of uncertainty in his eyes. She leaned forward, her voice softening. "Mr. Thompson, I can see this isn't easy for you. What's really holding you back?"

The man's shoulders sagged, and he suddenly looked much older. "You don't understand. Evelyn... she knew things. Things that could ruin people's careers, including mine."

Sarah nodded encouragingly. "I'm here to listen, not to judge. Whatever you tell me stays between us until it's absolutely necessary for the case."

Mr. Thompson ran a hand over his face. "God, where do I even start?"

Sarah's keen eyes noticed the slight tremor in Mr. Thompson's hands as he clasped them on the table. She glanced at Mrs. Jenkins, who sat quietly in the corner, her face pale and drawn. The tension in the room was palpable, thick enough to cut with a knife.

"Mr. Thompson, Mrs. Jenkins," Sarah began, her voice steady and reassuring, "I want you both to know that I understand your fears. They're valid, and I take them seriously."

She paused, observing their reactions. Mr. Thompson's jaw clenched, while Mrs. Jenkins nervously fidgeted with her necklace.

"The killer is still out there," Mrs. Jenkins whispered, her voice barely audible. "What if... what if they come after us next?"

Sarah leaned forward, her piercing gaze moving between the two witnesses. "That's exactly why your cooperation is crucial. The more information we have, the faster we can catch this person."

Mr. Thompson shook his head. "Easy for you to say, Detective. You're not the one risking everything."

Sarah's mind raced, considering their options. She'd seen witnesses clam up before, but rarely with such genuine fear. This called for a different approach.

"I have an idea," she said, her tone conveying confidence she didn't entirely feel. "We can arrange for your testimonies to be given anonymously. No names attached to the official record."

Mrs. Jenkins perked up slightly. "Is that... is that possible?"

"It's not standard procedure," Sarah admitted, "but I can make it happen. We could also discuss temporary relocation or protection if necessary."

Mr. Thompson's brow furrowed. "And how do we know we can trust you to follow through?"

Sarah met his gaze unflinchingly. "Because solving this case means as much to me as it does to you. I give you my word, and in my line of work, that's everything."

As she outlined her plan, Sarah could see the tension in the room slowly begin to dissipate. It wasn't a perfect solution, but it was a start. And sometimes, she reflected, that's all you need to break a case wide open.

Sarah leaned forward, her eyes moving between Mrs. Jenkins and Mr. Thompson. The fluorescent lights of the small conference room cast harsh shadows, emphasizing the worry lines on their faces.

"I understand your concerns," Sarah said, her voice steady and reassuring. "But your cooperation could be the key to solving Evelyn's murder. Here's what I propose: we'll set up a secure line for you to provide your statements. No names, no addresses. Just the facts as you remember them."

Mrs. Jenkins twisted her hands in her lap. "But what if someone figures out it was us?"

Sarah nodded, acknowledging the fear. "That's why we're also offering temporary relocation. A safe house, if necessary, until we apprehend the suspect."

Mr. Thompson scoffed, but Sarah could see a flicker of interest in his eyes. "And our jobs? Our lives? We can't just disappear."

"We'll work with your employers," Sarah assured him. "Create a cover story if needed. Your safety is our top priority."

Sarah felt a familiar determination rising within her. She'd been here before, coaxing reluctant witnesses into cooperation. But this time felt different. More personal.

"Look," she said, softening her tone. "I know I'm asking a lot. But think about Evelyn. Think about her family. They deserve closure, and you two hold pieces of the puzzle that could make that happen."

Mrs. Jenkins dabbed at her eyes with a tissue. "I... I want to help. I really do. But I'm so scared."

Sarah reached out, briefly touching the older woman's hand. "Fear is normal, Mrs. Jenkins. But courage isn't the absence of fear. It's acting in spite of it."

Mr. Thompson cleared his throat. "And you swear our names won't be attached to any of this?"

"You have my word," Sarah said firmly. "And in my years on the force, I've never broken that."

As Sarah's words hung in the air, a palpable shift in the atmosphere became evident. The once-tense shoulders of Mrs. Jenkins and Mr. Thompson began to relax, their furrowed brows smoothing out ever so slightly. The stuffy interrogation room seemed to lose some of its oppressive quality, the harsh fluorescent lights now casting a softer glow.

Mrs. Jenkins took a deep, shaky breath. "I... I think I can do this," she said, her voice trembling but resolute. The scent of her lavender perfume wafted through the air as she leaned forward, her eyes meeting Sarah's with newfound determination.

Mr. Thompson nodded slowly, the creases around his eyes softening. "If it means bringing justice for Evelyn... I suppose I'm in too."

Sarah felt a wave of relief wash over her, but she maintained her composed exterior. "Thank you both. Your courage will make a real difference."

Mrs. Jenkins clasped her hands together, a memory suddenly sparking in her eyes. "Oh! There's something else I remembered. That night, I saw the suspicious figure carrying something. It looked like... like a golf club."

Sarah's heart raced at this new information. "A golf club? Are you certain?"

Mrs. Jenkins nodded vigorously. "Yes, I'm sure of it now. I didn't think it was important before, but..."

"Every detail matters," Sarah assured her, jotting down notes. She turned to Mr. Thompson. "And you're willing to testify about your interactions with Evelyn leading up to that night?"

Mr. Thompson squared his shoulders. "I am. It's... it's the right thing to do."

As Sarah gathered her notes, a small smile played at the corners of her mouth. This was progress – real, tangible progress. The investigation was far from over, but for the first time in days, she felt a glimmer of hope.

"We'll be in touch soon to arrange the next steps," Sarah said, standing up. "Thank you both again. You've given us a fighting chance to solve this case."

Chapter 7

Kevin Johnson stepped into the bustling precinct, his crisp new uniform still stiff against his skin. The cacophony of ringing phones, shuffling papers, and overlapping conversations washed over him as he took a deep breath, steadying his nerves. This was it—his first day as a real police officer.

"You've got this, Kev," he muttered under his breath, squaring his shoulders. His eyes darted around the room, taking in the organized chaos of desks, bulletin boards covered in mugshots and maps, and harried-looking detectives hunched over case files.

As Kevin made his way towards the sergeant's desk to check in, he couldn't help but feel a surge of pride. He'd dreamed of this moment since he was a kid, listening to his dad's stories about life on the force. Now it was his turn to make a difference.

Across the room, Detective Sarah Mitchell glanced up from her paperwork, her sharp eyes zeroing in on the fresh-faced rookie. She watched as Kevin nervously adjusted his belt, a small smile tugging at the corner of her mouth. His eagerness was almost palpable, reminding her of her own first days on the job.

"Hey, Thompson," Sarah called out to a passing officer. "Who's the new kid?"

Officer Thompson paused, following Sarah's gaze. "Oh, that's Kevin Johnson. Just graduated from the academy last week. I hear he's got potential."

Sarah nodded, her interest piqued. "Is that so?" She studied Kevin more closely, noting the way he seemed to be absorbing every detail of his surroundings. There was an alertness in his stance, a keen intelligence in his eyes that went beyond mere rookie enthusiasm.

As Kevin approached the sergeant's desk, Sarah found herself rising from her chair. Maybe this was just what her investigation needed—a fresh perspective, untainted by years of cynicism and bureaucracy. She'd been hitting dead ends for weeks now, and a pair of new eyes might just spot something she'd overlooked.

"Well," Sarah mused to herself, "let's see what you're made of, Officer Johnson."

Sarah approached Kevin with confident strides, her piercing eyes fixed on the young officer. As she neared, Kevin's posture straightened, a mix of nervousness and excitement flickering across his face.

"Officer Johnson, isn't it?" Sarah extended her hand. "I'm Detective Sarah Mitchell."

Kevin's eyes widened in recognition. "Detective Mitchell! It's an honor to meet you, ma'am." He shook her hand firmly, his enthusiasm evident in his grip. "I've heard so much about your work."

Sarah's lips quirked into a half-smile. "Is that so? Well, I hope it wasn't all bad." She gestured towards a quieter corner of the bustling station. "Walk with me, Johnson. I'd like to hear more about you."

As they moved, Sarah observed Kevin's attentive gaze, taking in every detail of the station. She couldn't help but be reminded of her younger self.

"So, Johnson," Sarah began, her tone casual but probing, "what made you decide to join the force? Family tradition? Childhood dream?"

Kevin's face lit up. "Actually, it was your Riverside case that inspired me, Detective." He rubbed the back of his neck, a touch embarrassed. "I followed it closely in the papers. The way you pieced together those clues, it was... well, it was incredible. I knew then that this was what I wanted to do."

Sarah felt a warmth spread through her chest, touched by the sincerity in Kevin's voice. It had been a long time since she'd felt that kind of admiration from a colleague. "That case was a tough one," she admitted. "But it's good to know it had a positive impact."

Kevin nodded eagerly. "I've read about all your cases since then. The way you approach each one, it's like... like solving a complex puzzle. I'd love to learn from you, if you'd be willing to share some insights."

Sarah studied Kevin for a moment, weighing his words. There was a genuine hunger for knowledge in his eyes, a desire to make a difference that resonated with her own motivations for joining the force years ago.

"Well, Johnson," she said, a hint of amusement in her voice, "flattery will get you everywhere. But be careful what you wish for. My methods aren't always by the book."

Kevin's eyes sparkled with excitement. "I'm ready to learn, Detective. Whatever it takes to become half the detective you are."

Sarah chuckled, shaking her head. "Alright, rookie. Let's see if you can put your money where your mouth is. I might just have a task for you..."

Sarah leaned against her desk, her eyes narrowing as she studied Kevin. The overhead fluorescent lights flickered, casting shadows across her face and accentuating the intensity of her gaze.

"Alright, Johnson," she said, her voice low and serious. "We've got a case that's been giving us hell. Young woman found dead in her apartment, no signs of forced entry. On the surface, it looks like suicide, but something doesn't add up."

Kevin's posture straightened, his eyes widening with interest. "What makes you think it's not suicide, Detective?"

Sarah's lips curved into a slight smile, pleased by his quick uptake. "Good question. The victim, Emily Reeves, had just landed her dream job and was planning a trip to Europe. Not exactly the actions of someone contemplating ending their life."

She paused, running a hand through her hair. "But here's where it gets complicated. We need to dig deeper into Emily's past, her relationships. And for that, we need more hands on deck."

Kevin nodded eagerly. "I'm ready to help in any way I can, Detective."

Sarah's response was cut short by the sound of the station door opening. A woman with warm brown eyes and auburn hair stepped inside, her gaze scanning the room before landing on Sarah.

"Speaking of help," Sarah murmured, straightening up. "Kevin, I'd like you to meet Linda Carter. She's a social worker who's been invaluable in past cases."

As Linda approached, Sarah couldn't help but notice the stark contrast between the newcomer's soft, earthy-toned clothing and the harsh, sterile environment of the police station. It was like a breath of fresh air in the midst of their grim surroundings.

"Linda," Sarah called out, raising a hand in greeting. "Thanks for coming in. We've got quite the puzzle on our hands, and I think your perspective might be just what we need."

Linda's face lit up with a warm smile as she approached Sarah and Kevin. "Always happy to help, Sarah," she said, her voice gentle yet filled with genuine enthusiasm. She extended her hand to Kevin, her eyes crinkling at the corners. "And you must be the new officer I've been hearing about. It's a pleasure to meet you, Kevin."

Kevin shook her hand firmly, his posture straightening almost imperceptibly. "The pleasure's all mine, Ms. Carter. I've heard great things about your work with the department."

Sarah watched the interaction, a hint of a smile tugging at her lips. She could already see Linda's natural warmth putting Kevin at ease, softening the edges of his eager-to-impress demeanor.

"Linda has a knack for getting people to open up," Sarah explained, her tone matter-of-fact but tinged with respect. "Her insights have been crucial in several cases."

Linda waved off the compliment with a modest gesture. "Oh, I just listen. Sometimes that's all people need - someone to really hear them." She turned to Sarah, her expression growing more serious. "So, what can I do to help with this case? It sounds like you could use an extra pair of ears."

Sarah nodded, her mind already racing with possibilities. "Your empathy could be invaluable here, Linda. We need to understand our victim's mindset, her relationships. There's more to this story than what's on the surface."

As Linda nodded her understanding, Kevin couldn't help but interject, his curiosity getting the better of him. "Ms. Carter, how do you approach these sensitive situations? It must be challenging to balance empathy with the need for information."

Linda's eyes sparkled at the question. "That's an excellent point, Kevin. It's all about creating a safe space for people to share their truths. Sometimes, the smallest details can be the most important."

Sarah's eyes darted between Linda and Kevin, her analytical mind already piecing together a strategy. She leaned forward, her voice dropping to a confidential tone.

"Linda, our victim, Melissa Thompson, led a complex life. On the surface, she was a successful real estate agent, but we've uncovered some inconsistencies in her personal relationships. I need your expertise to help us understand her motivations, her fears, her hopes. What might have led her into a dangerous situation?"

Linda nodded thoughtfully, her warm brown eyes filled with compassion. "Of course, Sarah. Sometimes people wear masks to protect themselves, but those masks can also attract the wrong kind of attention. I'd be happy to review her background and maybe speak with her friends and family."

Sarah felt a familiar spark of excitement, the kind that always ignited when a case started to come together. She glanced at Kevin, noticing his eager expression, then back to Linda.

"I've been thinking," Sarah said, her tone cautious but determined. "This case requires a multi-faceted approach. Kevin's fresh perspective, Linda's empathy and insight, and my investigative experience... We could form quite an effective team."

Kevin's eyes widened, and Sarah could practically see the wheels turning in his mind. Linda's face lit up with a gentle smile.

"That's a wonderful idea, Sarah," Linda said, her voice warm with enthusiasm. "Combining our different strengths could really make a difference. And I'm sure Kevin here has some unique insights to offer as well."

Sarah nodded, allowing herself a small smile. "Exactly. Kevin's training is up-to-date, and his eagerness to learn could be a real asset. Plus, having a uniformed officer on the team might make some witnesses more comfortable."

As Sarah outlined her vision for their collaboration, she couldn't help but feel a twinge of her usual caution. Trusting others didn't come easily to her, but she knew that to crack this case, she needed to take that risk.

Kevin leaned forward, his eyes bright with excitement. "Detective Mitchell, I can't tell you how much this means to me," he said, his voice brimming with enthusiasm. "Working alongside professionals like you and Ms. Carter... it's an incredible opportunity."

Sarah noticed Kevin's hands fidgeting slightly, betraying his nervous energy. She remembered feeling that same mix of excitement and anxiety early in her own career.

"I promise I'll give it my all," Kevin continued earnestly. "I may be new, but I'm a quick learner, and I'm ready to contribute in any way I can."

Linda reached out and patted Kevin's arm gently. "That's the spirit, Kevin. Your enthusiasm is exactly what we need on this team."

Sarah nodded, allowing herself a small smile. She appreciated Kevin's eagerness, even if part of her worried it might lead to mistakes. Still, his energy was infectious, and she found herself feeling more optimistic about their chances of solving the case.

Linda turned to Sarah, her warm brown eyes reflecting determination. "Count me in, Sarah. These victims deserve justice, and if my expertise can help in any way, I'm all in."

Sarah felt a wave of relief wash over her. Linda's empathy and understanding of human nature would be invaluable in navigating the complex web of relationships surrounding the victim.

"Thank you, Linda," Sarah said, her usually guarded tone softening slightly. "Your insight will be crucial in understanding the victim's background and potential motives of those close to her."

As the three of them sat there, the buzz of the police station fading into the background, Sarah felt a tentative spark of hope. It had been a long time since she'd allowed herself to rely on others, but looking at Kevin's eager face and Linda's compassionate smile, she thought that maybe, just maybe, this team could make a real difference.

Sarah leaned forward, her piercing eyes scanning Kevin and Linda's faces. "Alright, let's break this down," she said, her voice crisp and focused. "Kevin, I want you to handle the legwork. Canvas the neighborhood, talk to potential witnesses. Your fresh perspective might uncover details we've missed."

Kevin nodded eagerly, his pen poised over his notepad. Sarah could almost see the wheels turning in his head, and she hoped his enthusiasm wouldn't blind him to potential dangers.

"Linda," Sarah continued, turning to the social worker, "your role is crucial. I need you to dig into the victim's background. Family dynamics, relationships, any potential conflicts. Your expertise in reading people will be invaluable."

Linda's warm eyes met Sarah's. "I understand. I'll start by reaching out to her closest contacts, see what I can uncover about her personal life."

Sarah nodded, a mixture of determination and caution swirling in her mind. "Remember, we're a team now. Share everything you find, no matter how insignificant it might seem. Trust me, in cases like these, the devil's in the details."

Kevin cleared his throat. "So, what's our first move, Detective Mitchell?"

Sarah allowed herself a small smile at his eagerness. "We start by building a comprehensive timeline. Kevin, I want you to gather surveillance footage from businesses near the crime scene. Linda, can you start compiling a list of the victim's known associates?"

As they discussed their next steps, Sarah felt a familiar tension in her shoulders ease slightly. Maybe, just maybe, this collaborative approach could work. But a nagging voice in the back of her mind whispered caution. Trust, but verify. Always verify.

Sarah took a deep breath, feeling a surge of energy as she looked at her newly-formed team. Kevin's eyes shone with enthusiasm, while Linda's calm demeanor radiated reassurance. The detective allowed herself a moment of cautious optimism.

"Alright, team," Sarah said, her voice steady and determined. "Let's wrap this up and get moving. We've got a long road ahead, but I believe we're on the right track."

Kevin nodded vigorously, barely containing his excitement. "I can't wait to get started on that surveillance footage, Detective Mitchell. I'll comb through every second if that's what it takes."

Sarah couldn't help but smile at his eagerness. "Just remember, Kevin, patience is key. Don't burn yourself out on the first day."

Linda chimed in, her tone warm but practical. "I've got a few contacts who might be able to shed some light on our victim's background. I'll start reaching out first thing tomorrow morning."

As they gathered their belongings, Sarah felt a spark of hope ignite within her. It had been a long time since she'd allowed herself to feel this way about a case or a team. The familiar walls of self-reliance seemed to waver slightly.

"Before we go," Sarah said, her voice softer than usual, "I want you both to know that I appreciate your commitment to this case. It won't be easy, but together, we might just have a shot at cracking it."

Kevin beamed at her words, while Linda offered a gentle, understanding smile. As they filed out of the conference room, Sarah found herself trailing behind, lost in thought.

Maybe this time will be different, she mused, allowing herself a moment of vulnerability. Maybe this team could be the key to unlocking not just the case, but something within herself as well.

With a mix of anticipation and trepidation, Sarah switched off the lights and closed the door behind her, ready to face whatever challenges lay ahead – this time, not alone, but as part of a team.

Chapter 8

Detective Sarah Mitchell stepped into Evelyn Langdon's immaculate living room, her keen eyes scanning every detail. The air was heavy with the scent of lemon furniture polish and old money.

"Alright team, let's be thorough," Sarah instructed, her voice steady despite the weight of the case. "We're looking for anything that might shed light on Evelyn's relationship with her son."

As her colleagues spread out, Sarah found herself drawn to a pristine bookshelf. She ran a gloved finger along the spines, noting the titles were all perfectly aligned. Everything in its place, she thought. Just like Evelyn herself.

Her gaze fell on a framed photo of Robert and Evelyn. The mother's smile was tight, her hand gripping her son's shoulder. Robert's expression was harder to read - a mix of charm and something darker.

What was really going on between you two? Sarah wondered, carefully lifting the frame.

"Detective Mitchell," called one of her team members. "You might want to see this."

Sarah crossed the room, her sensible shoes sinking into the plush carpet. On an antique writing desk sat a stack of social engagement cards, each one meticulously filled out in Evelyn's elegant script.

"Looks like Mrs. Langdon kept a busy social calendar," Sarah mused aloud.

"Yeah, but check this out," her colleague pointed to several crossed-out entries. "All of these were events Robert was supposed to attend with her."

Sarah's brow furrowed. "Interesting. Make sure we get photos of all of these."

As her team continued their methodical search, Sarah's mind raced. The immaculate home seemed to be full of secrets, just waiting to be uncovered.

Later that afternoon, Sarah found herself seated across from Margaret Holloway, Evelyn's closest friend for over three decades. The elderly woman's hands trembled slightly as she lifted her teacup.

"Mrs. Holloway," Sarah began gently, "can you tell me about Evelyn's relationship with Robert?"

Margaret's eyes darted nervously. "Oh, well, Evelyn always wanted the best for Robert. She had such high hopes for him."

"And how did Robert respond to those expectations?"

Margaret hesitated, then sighed. "Robert...he tried. He really did. But sometimes, it seemed like nothing he did was ever quite good enough for Evelyn."

Sarah leaned forward, her interest piqued. "Can you give me an example?"

"Well," Margaret lowered her voice, as if sharing a secret, "there was this time Robert won a prestigious award at work. Most mothers would have been over the moon, but Evelyn...she just asked why it wasn't the top prize."

Sarah nodded, making a mental note. "How did Robert handle that kind of criticism?"

"He always put on a brave face," Margaret replied, her voice tinged with sadness. "But sometimes, I'd catch a look in his eyes...a sort of desperate unhappiness. It broke my heart, really."

As Margaret continued to speak, Sarah felt the pieces of the puzzle slowly starting to come together. The perfect facade of the Langdon family was beginning to crack, revealing the complex, troubled relationship beneath.

This case is far from straightforward, Sarah thought, her mind already planning the next steps of the investigation. But then again, when are they ever?

Sarah's fingers traced the edge of Evelyn's mahogany desk, her keen eyes scanning for anything out of place. As she pressed against a seemingly innocuous panel, a soft click echoed through the room.

"What do we have here?" Sarah muttered, her heart quickening as a hidden compartment sprung open.

Inside lay a stack of leather-bound journals, their spines cracked from frequent use. Sarah lifted one out, the weight of secrets heavy in her hands.

"Hey, Carter," she called to her partner. "I think I've found something interesting."

As Carter approached, Sarah flipped open the first journal, her eyes widening at the meticulous handwriting that filled each page.

"Evelyn's journals," she breathed. "This could be exactly what we need."

Sarah began to read, her brow furrowing as she delved into Evelyn's innermost thoughts. The pristine image of the poised matriarch began to crumble with each turn of the page.

"God, listen to this," Sarah said, her voice a mix of disbelief and fascination. "'Robert's presentation was adequate, but hardly befitting a Langdon. When will he learn to truly excel?'"

Carter whistled low. "Tough crowd."

Sarah nodded, flipping through more pages. "It gets worse. Here's an entry from Robert's 30th birthday: 'Another year, and still no significant achievements to speak of. I fear I've failed as a mother.'"

As she read on, Sarah felt a knot forming in her stomach. The journals painted a picture of a woman consumed by perfection, her love for her son tangled up in impossible expectations.

"I can't imagine living under this kind of pressure," Sarah murmured, more to herself than to Carter. She thought of her own childhood, filled with encouragement rather than criticism. How different would she be if every action had been scrutinized and found wanting?

Carter leaned against the desk, his face grim. "No wonder Robert always seemed so... tense around his mother. This is psychological warfare."

Sarah nodded, her mind racing. "We need to dig deeper into Robert's life. These journals might just be the key to understanding the dynamics at play here."

As she closed the journal, Sarah couldn't shake the image of Robert – charming, successful Robert – carrying the weight of his mother's disappointment. It was a stark reminder that even the most polished exteriors could hide deep-seated pain.

"Let's get these back to the station," Sarah said, carefully gathering the journals. "We've got a lot of reading ahead of us."

Detective Sarah Mitchell's phone buzzed insistently, pulling her attention away from Evelyn's journals. She glanced at the screen, her eyebrows rising as she read the message from her colleague, Detective Rodriguez.

"Carter," she called out, her voice tight with anticipation. "Rodriguez just uncovered something big on John Blackwood. We need to head back to the station."

The drive back was a blur of traffic lights and Sarah's racing thoughts. As soon as they arrived, she strode purposefully towards the conference room, where Rodriguez was waiting with a stack of files.

"What have you got?" Sarah asked, her piercing eyes fixed on her colleague.

Rodriguez spread out several documents on the table. "John Blackwood isn't just some random hitman. He's got a rap sheet longer than my arm. Burglary, assault, suspected involvement in at least two other murders... This guy's been dancing on the edge of the law for years."

Sarah leaned in, her fingers tracing the lines of a particularly detailed police report. "Any known associates?"

"That's where it gets interesting," Rodriguez replied, a hint of excitement in his voice. "I've set up interviews with a few of his former... colleagues. One of them, a guy named Mickey 'The Rat' Thompson, is waiting in Interview Room 2 right now."

Sarah nodded, her mind already formulating questions. As she headed towards the interview room, she couldn't help but wonder about the enigmatic John Blackwood. What had driven him to this life? And more importantly, how had he crossed paths with Robert?

She paused at the door, taking a deep breath to center herself. Interviews like these could make or break a case, and she needed to be at the top of her game. With one last steadying breath, she pushed open the door and stepped inside.

Mickey 'The Rat' Thompson looked up as she entered, his watery eyes darting nervously around the room. Sarah sat down across from him, her posture relaxed but her gaze intense.

"Mr. Thompson," she began, her voice calm but authoritative. "I appreciate you coming in to talk with us about John Blackwood."

Mickey shifted uncomfortably in his seat. "Yeah, well, I ain't exactly here by choice, am I? What d'you wanna know about Johnny?"

Sarah leaned forward slightly. "Tell me about your history with him. How did you two meet?"

As Mickey began to speak, Sarah listened intently, her mind piecing together the puzzle of John Blackwood's past. With each revelation, she felt herself getting closer to understanding the man behind the murder – and perhaps, to unraveling the entire twisted plot that had led to Evelyn's death.

Detective Sarah Mitchell rubbed her tired eyes as she pored over the stack of financial records spread across her desk. The fluorescent lights in the precinct buzzed overhead, casting a harsh glow on the papers before her.

"Holy shit," she muttered, sitting bolt upright. "Guys, come look at this!"

Her team members hurried over, crowding around her desk. Sarah pointed to a series of transactions highlighted in yellow.

"See these payments? They're from Robert to an offshore account. And look at the dates - they line up perfectly with John's known movements."

Detective Johnson leaned in, squinting at the numbers. "You think Robert was bankrolling John?"

Sarah nodded grimly. "It sure looks that way. And there's more - large withdrawals from Evelyn's accounts right before her death."

"Damn," whispered Detective Ramirez. "So Robert might've been more involved than we thought."

Sarah leaned back in her chair, her mind racing. "We need to brainstorm this. What could've driven Robert to get mixed up in all this?"

Johnson perched on the edge of the desk. "Well, we know he and Evelyn had a strained relationship. Maybe he just snapped?"

"It's more than that," Sarah mused, tapping her pen against her chin. "Remember how his secretary described him? Always trying to impress Evelyn, always falling short."

Ramirez nodded. "The pressure of those expectations... it could drive anyone to extremes."

Sarah stood up, pacing as she thought out loud. "So we've got a son desperate to prove himself, a mother with impossibly high standards, and a hired gun with a shady past. What if Robert saw this as his last chance to finally measure up?"

"By orchestrating his own mother's murder?" Johnson asked incredulously.

Sarah shrugged. "It's twisted, but it fits. He gets rid of the source of his misery and inherits a fortune in one fell swoop."

As the team continued to debate theories, Sarah couldn't shake the image of Robert's polished exterior cracking under the weight of his mother's disapproval. What dark secrets lay beneath that perfect façade?

Sarah's piercing gaze swept across her cluttered desk, landing on Dr. Elizabeth Shaw's business card. She picked it up, running her thumb over the embossed lettering.

"Time to bring in an expert," she muttered, reaching for her phone.

As she dialed, Sarah's mind raced with questions. What hidden depths lay beneath the surface of the Langdon family drama? She needed answers, and Dr. Shaw might be the key to unlocking them.

The phone rang twice before a warm, authoritative voice answered. "Dr. Elizabeth Shaw speaking."

"Dr. Shaw, this is Detective Sarah Mitchell. I'm working on a case that could use your expertise. Do you have time to meet?"

There was a brief pause. "Of course, Detective. I always make time for intriguing cases. Shall we say tomorrow at 2 PM?"

Sarah felt a surge of relief. "Perfect. I'll bring our files to your office."

As she hung up, Sarah couldn't help but wonder what insights Dr. Shaw might provide. Would she be able to shed light on the twisted relationship between Evelyn and Robert?

The next day, Sarah found herself seated across from Dr. Shaw in a cozy office lined with bookshelves. The psychologist's silver-streaked hair framed a face etched with both wisdom and kindness.

"So, Detective Mitchell," Dr. Shaw began, leaning forward slightly, "tell me about this case that's troubling you."

Sarah took a deep breath. "It's a murder investigation, but it's the family dynamics that have us stumped. We have a controlling mother, a son desperate for approval, and a web of resentment that might have led to murder."

Dr. Shaw's eyes lit up with interest. "Intriguing indeed. Let's start with the mother. What can you tell me about her?"

As Sarah described Evelyn's imperious nature and exacting standards, she noticed Dr. Shaw nodding thoughtfully, her fingers steepled under her chin.

"And Robert?" Dr. Shaw prompted. "How did he respond to his mother's expectations?"

Sarah frowned, recalling the image of Robert's polished exterior. "On the surface, he seemed like the perfect son. But underneath... there was this constant strain, this need to prove himself."

Dr. Shaw leaned back, a look of understanding crossing her face. "What we're dealing with here, Detective, is a classic case of toxic family dynamics. Evelyn's controlling behavior likely stemmed from her own insecurities, but it created an environment where Robert felt he could never measure up."

Sarah felt a chill run down her spine. "Could that really drive someone to murder?"

"In extreme cases, absolutely," Dr. Shaw replied, her tone grave. "When someone has spent their entire life trying to win an unwinnable game, they may see drastic action as their only escape."

As Dr. Shaw continued to explain the psychological intricacies of the case, Sarah found herself scribbling notes furiously. With each insight, she felt like she was peeling back another layer of the mystery.

"Remember, Detective," Dr. Shaw said as their meeting drew to a close, "understanding these dynamics is crucial. It's not just about what happened, but why it happened."

Sarah nodded, her mind already racing with new angles to pursue. As she gathered her files, she couldn't shake the feeling that she was finally on the right track. The truth was within reach – she just had to keep digging.

Sarah strode into the precinct, the weight of Dr. Shaw's insights heavy on her mind. The bullpen buzzed with activity, but she barely noticed as she made her way to the conference room where her team waited.

"Alright, let's regroup," Sarah announced, dropping her files on the table with a satisfying thud. She looked around at her team's expectant faces, their eyes reflecting a mix of exhaustion and determination.

Detective Rodriguez leaned forward, his chair creaking. "What did the shrink say?"

Sarah took a deep breath, her fingers drumming on the table. "Dr. Shaw confirmed our suspicions about the dysfunctional relationship between Robert and Evelyn. It's worse than we thought."

"How so?" Detective Chen asked, her brow furrowed.

"We're dealing with years of psychological manipulation," Sarah explained, her voice tight. "Robert's entire life has been a pressure cooker. Dr. Shaw thinks it could have driven him to extreme measures."

The room fell silent as the implications sank in. Sarah's mind raced, considering their next move. We need more, she thought. Suspicions aren't enough. We need hard evidence.

"Okay, team," Sarah said, breaking the silence. "We need to focus on gathering more concrete evidence. Rodriguez, I want you to dig deeper into Robert's financials. Chen, coordinate with forensics - there might be something we missed at the crime scene."

"What about you, boss?" Rodriguez asked, already pulling out his phone.

Sarah's eyes narrowed with determination. "I'm going to have another chat with Robert's colleagues. Someone must have noticed something off about his behavior leading up to Evelyn's murder."

As her team dispersed, Sarah found herself staring at the evidence board. Robert's charming smile looked back at her from his photograph, and she couldn't help but wonder what secrets lay behind those seemingly warm eyes.

"We're coming for you, Robert," she murmured, her resolve strengthening. "No matter how deep you've buried the truth, we'll find it."

With a final glance at the board, Sarah grabbed her jacket and headed for the door. The truth was out there, waiting to be uncovered, and she was determined to bring Evelyn the justice she deserved.

Chapter 9

The harsh blue glow of the computer screen illuminated Sarah's face as she scrolled through her inbox. Her eyes narrowed, focusing on a new message from an unfamiliar address. As she clicked to open it, a chill ran down her spine.

"Back off the investigation now, or you'll regret it. This is your only warning."

Sarah's breath caught in her throat, her heart rate quickening. She re-read the message, analyzing every word. The threat was clear, but vague enough to leave her imagination running wild. Her fingers hovered over the keyboard, mind racing.

"Not a chance," she muttered, pushing back from her desk. The wheels of her chair squeaked against the linoleum floor as she stood, grabbing her phone.

Sarah paced the small office, dialing her team while glancing periodically at the ominous message still displayed on her screen. "Everyone, my office. Now," she said curtly before hanging up.

Within minutes, her team filed in, expressions curious and concerned.

"What's going on, boss?" Detective Rodriguez asked, leaning against the doorframe.

Sarah took a deep breath, steeling herself. "I just received a threat. Anonymous email warning me to back off the case."

A chorus of surprised murmurs filled the room. Sarah held up a hand, silencing them.

"Listen, I know this is serious, but we can't let it derail us. We're too close to cracking this case wide open."

Officer Chen stepped forward, her brow furrowed. "But Sarah, shouldn't we take this to Internal Affairs? What if it's not just an empty threat?"

Sarah shook her head, a wry smile tugging at her lips. "And risk them pulling us off the case? Not a chance. We've come too far."

She could see the concern in their eyes, mirroring her own internal struggle. But beneath that worry, she recognized the determination that had made her choose each of them for her team.

"Alright, let's think this through," Sarah said, pacing again. "What are our options for protecting ourselves without compromising the investigation?"

Detective Rodriguez spoke up, "We could increase security protocols, maybe set up a buddy system so no one's working alone."

Sarah nodded, her mind already racing ahead. "Good. Chen, I want you to do a deep dive on that email. See if we can trace its origin."

As her team brainstormed, Sarah felt a familiar fire igniting within her. Every obstacle only fueled her determination. She'd faced threats before, survived loss and betrayal. This case – this victim – deserved justice, and she'd be damned if an anonymous coward would stop her from delivering it.

"Whatever happens," Sarah said, her voice steady and strong, "we stick together. We watch each other's backs. And we do not back down. Understood?"

A chorus of affirmatives filled the room, and Sarah felt a surge of pride. She may work best alone, but in moments like these, she was grateful for the unwavering support of her team.

"Alright," she said, a hint of a smile playing at her lips. "Let's show this bastard what happens when you threaten the wrong detective."

Sarah's boots crunched on broken glass as she stepped through the shattered sliding door of Evelyn's apartment. The crime scene, previously processed, now felt different under the weight of the anonymous threat. Sarah's eyes darted around, hyperaware of every shadow and sound.

"Fan out," she instructed her team, her voice low and measured. "Document everything. No detail is too small."

As her colleagues spread through the apartment, Sarah moved methodically, her piercing gaze scrutinizing every surface. The faint scent of copper still lingered in the air, a grim reminder of the violence that had occurred here.

"Mitchell," Detective Rodriguez called from the kitchen, his voice tense. "You need to see this."

Sarah strode over, her heart rate quickening. On the pristine white tile of the backsplash, a stark crimson handprint stood out like an accusation.

"How did we miss this before?" Sarah muttered, more to herself than anyone else. Her mind raced, considering the implications. Was this new? Or had they overlooked it in their initial sweep?

"It wasn't here before," Chen said, echoing Sarah's thoughts. "I photographed this area myself."

Sarah's jaw clenched. "Someone's been here since we processed the scene. And they're taunting us."

She took a deep breath, pushing down the unease crawling up her spine. "Alright, listen up," she called out, her voice steady and authoritative. "We've got new evidence. I want this documented meticulously. Chen, get photos from every angle. Rodriguez, start on the fingerprint analysis. Johnson, sweep the surrounding area for any other disturbances."

As her team sprang into action, Sarah stood back, watching their efficiency with a mixture of pride and concern. She couldn't shake the feeling that they were being watched, tested.

"What's your game?" she whispered, her eyes locked on the bloody handprint. "What are you trying to tell us?"

Sarah's phone vibrated in her pocket, cutting through the tense atmosphere. She pulled it out, frowning at the unknown number. Her instincts screamed caution, but curiosity won out.

"Detective Mitchell," she answered, her voice clipped and professional.

A distorted, mechanical voice crackled through the speaker. "You're digging too deep, Detective. Back off now, or you'll be sorry."

Sarah's grip on the phone tightened, her knuckles turning white. "Who is this?" she demanded, even as her team's heads snapped up at her tone.

"Consider this your final warning," the voice continued, ignoring her question. "Drop the case, or there will be consequences."

The line went dead.

Sarah lowered the phone slowly, her mind racing. Anger bubbled up inside her, mixing with frustration and a hint of fear she refused to acknowledge.

"Everything okay, boss?" Rodriguez asked, concern etching his features.

Sarah took a deep breath, squaring her shoulders. "Just another attempt to scare us off," she said, her voice steady. "But we're not backing down. Let's finish up here and head back to the station. We've got work to do."

An hour later, Sarah stood before the evidence board at the precinct, her team gathered around her. The bloody handprint, now photographed and analyzed, took center stage.

"Alright, what do we know?" Sarah asked, her piercing gaze sweeping over her colleagues.

Chen stepped forward, gesturing to the image. "The print doesn't match any in our database, but the size and shape suggest it's likely male."

"And its connection to John Blackwood?" Sarah pressed, her mind immediately jumping to their prime suspect.

Rodriguez cleared his throat. "It's circumstantial at best. We can't definitively tie it to him without more evidence."

Sarah nodded, her brow furrowing. "What about alternative theories? Could this be someone trying to frame Blackwood?"

"It's possible," Johnson chimed in. "But why go to such lengths? And why now, after we've already processed the scene?"

The room fell silent as they pondered the implications. Sarah's mind raced, piecing together the puzzle. John Blackwood's enigmatic presence loomed large in her thoughts, his guarded demeanor and mysterious past raising more questions than answers.

"We're missing something," Sarah muttered, her eyes locked on the handprint. "This feels like a message, not just evidence. But what is it trying to tell us?"

Sarah's phone buzzed, pulling her from her thoughts. A text from Dr. Elizabeth Shaw: "Got a minute to talk?"

"I need some air," Sarah announced to her team. "Keep digging. I'll be back soon."

She found Dr. Shaw waiting in her office, a gentle smile on her face. "Sarah, how are you holding up?"

Sarah sank into a chair, the weight of the case pressing down on her. "Honestly? I'm not sure. These threats, the bloody handprint... it's all starting to feel personal."

Dr. Shaw leaned forward, her eyes kind but searching. "Tell me about the threats. What do you think they mean?"

"They want me to back off," Sarah said, her jaw tightening. "But why? What are they afraid we'll find?"

"Often, threats like these come from a place of fear," Dr. Shaw mused. "Our killer might be feeling cornered, desperate. It's a sign you're getting close."

Sarah nodded, considering. "And the handprint?"

"A taunt, perhaps. Or a challenge," Dr. Shaw suggested. "Either way, it's a deliberate act. Our killer is intelligent, methodical. They're playing a game, Sarah, and they want you to know it."

Sarah's fists clenched involuntarily. "So what do I do? How do I outsmart someone who's always one step ahead?"

Dr. Shaw's voice softened. "Trust your instincts, Sarah. They've gotten you this far. You have a gift for seeing what others miss. Use it."

Sarah felt a flicker of doubt. "But what if I'm wrong? What if I can't protect my team?"

"Doubt is natural," Dr. Shaw assured her. "But don't let it paralyze you. Your team trusts you. They believe in you. Now you need to believe in yourself."

Sarah stood, pacing the small office. "Evelyn deserves justice. Her family deserves answers. I can't let them down."

Dr. Shaw's eyes followed her. "And you won't. But remember, Sarah, you're not alone in this. Lean on your team, on your support system. That's where true strength comes from."

Sarah paused, feeling a renewed sense of determination. "You're right. Thank you, Dr. Shaw. I needed this."

As she left the office, Sarah's mind raced with new possibilities. The case wasn't just about evidence anymore. It was a battle of wills, a psychological game. And Sarah was determined to win.

Sarah's eyes burned as she stared intently at the flickering screen, the grainy surveillance footage playing on a loop. The dimly lit room buzzed with tension, her team huddled around her, their faces illuminated by the eerie glow of the monitor.

"There!" Detective Martinez exclaimed, pointing at a shadowy figure crossing the frame. "Rewind it, Sarah."

Sarah's fingers flew over the keyboard, rewinding the footage. Her heart raced as she studied the figure's gait, searching for any distinguishing features. "It could be our guy, but it's hard to tell. The quality is terrible."

"Can we enhance it?" Officer Chen asked, leaning in closer.

Sarah shook her head, frustration creeping into her voice. "We've tried. This is as good as it gets."

As they continued to scrutinize the footage, Sarah's phone buzzed in her pocket. She glanced at the screen, her brow furrowing at the unknown number.

"I need to take this," she muttered, stepping away from the group.

"Detective Mitchell," she answered, her voice low and cautious.

A distorted voice crackled through the speaker. "John Blackwood isn't who you think he is. Look into his connections with the Riverdale Syndicate."

Sarah's pulse quickened. "Who is this? How do you know-"

The line went dead.

She stood frozen for a moment, her mind racing. The Riverdale Syndicate? That was a name she hadn't expected to hear in connection with this case.

"Everything okay, boss?" Martinez called out, noticing her expression.

Sarah turned back to her team, her face a mask of determination. "We might have a new lead. John Blackwood may have ties to the Riverdale Syndicate."

The room erupted in murmurs of surprise and speculation.

"The Riverdale Syndicate?" Chen whistled low. "That's big-time organized crime. How'd you get that intel?"

Sarah hesitated, weighing her words carefully. "An anonymous tip. We can't trust it completely, but it's worth looking into."

She could feel the energy in the room shift, a renewed sense of purpose filling the air. Despite the potential danger, Sarah felt a surge of excitement. This could be the break they needed.

"Alright, team," she said, her voice steady and commanding. "Let's dig into this. I want everything we can find on the Syndicate and any possible connections to Blackwood. And keep this quiet for now. If this checks out, we could be dealing with something much bigger than we initially thought."

As her team sprang into action, Sarah cast one last glance at the paused surveillance footage. The shadowy figure seemed to stare back at her, taunting her with its secrets. She narrowed her eyes, a silent promise passing through her mind.

"I'm coming for you," she thought. "No matter who you are or who you're connected to. I will find the truth."

Sarah's heels clicked against the pavement as she approached the run-down apartment complex. The peeling paint and rusted railings spoke volumes about the neighborhood's struggles. Her team fanned out behind her, eyes scanning for potential threats.

"Remember," Sarah said, her voice low but firm, "these witnesses might be scared. We need to be gentle but persistent."

She rapped on the first door, paint flakes dusting her knuckles. A woman with tired eyes and a wary expression peered out.

"Mrs. Rodriguez?" Sarah asked, flashing her badge. "I'm Detective Mitchell. We'd like to ask you a few questions about the night of September 15th."

Mrs. Rodriguez's eyes darted nervously. "I don't know nothing," she muttered, starting to close the door.

Sarah's foot wedged in the gap. "Please," she said, softening her tone. "Anything you saw could help us catch a killer. We can protect you."

The woman hesitated, then relented. "I saw a man," she whispered. "Tall, scruffy. He was arguing with someone in a car. But I can't say more. They'll hurt my family."

Sarah's mind raced. Could this be John? "I understand your fear," she said gently. "But staying silent only protects the guilty. Help us make your neighborhood safer."

As they moved from door to door, Sarah felt the weight of each reluctant testimony, each fearful glance. The pieces were there, just out of reach.

Back at the station, she stared at the evidence board, her reflection ghostly in the glass. The anonymous threats, the bloody handprint, John's possible gang connections – it all swirled in her mind.

"I know you're out there," she murmured, her resolve hardening. "And I won't stop until I find you, no matter the cost."

Her phone buzzed. An unknown number. Sarah's heart raced as she answered.

A distorted voice crackled through the speaker: "You're getting too close, Detective. Back off, or the next body will be yours."

The line went dead, leaving Sarah with a chill running down her spine and a fire igniting in her eyes.

Chapter 10

The fluorescent lights buzzed overhead as Detective Sarah Mitchell leaned over the cluttered table, her eyes scanning the jumble of documents spread before her. The makeshift office, a repurposed storage room at the precinct, felt claustrophobic with her team crammed around her, their faces etched with determination.

"Anything new, Collins?" Sarah asked, her voice tight with frustration. She'd been staring at the same bank statement for what felt like hours, willing it to reveal its secrets.

Officer Collins shook his head, running a hand through his thinning hair. "Nothing yet, boss. But we're still combing through Evelyn's personal effects."

Sarah nodded, her gaze drifting back to the papers in front of her. A familiar knot of tension formed in her stomach as she thought about Robert Langdon, the prime suspect in his wife's murder. Something about him didn't sit right with her, but she couldn't quite put her finger on it.

As she shuffled through another stack of bank statements, a number caught her eye. Sarah blinked, certain she must be seeing things. She pulled the document closer, her heart beginning to race.

"Hey, guys," she said, her voice barely above a whisper. "I think I've got something."

The room fell silent as her team gathered around, their curiosity palpable. Sarah pointed to the statement, her finger trembling slightly.

"Look at this transfer," she said, tapping the paper. "Fifty thousand dollars from Robert's account to... John Blackwood."

Officer Rodriguez let out a low whistle. "That's a hefty sum. Any idea who this John character is?"

Sarah's mind raced, piecing together fragments of information. "John Blackwood... he's that drifter we interviewed last week.

Remember? The one with the intense stare who barely said two words?"

"Oh yeah," Collins chimed in. "Gave me the creeps, that one."

Sarah nodded, her thoughts whirling. What connection could there possibly be between the polished, upper-class Robert Langdon and the rough-around-the-edges John Blackwood? And why would Robert be transferring such a large sum of money to him?

As the implications began to sink in, Sarah felt a familiar surge of adrenaline. They were onto something big, she could feel it in her bones. But she forced herself to remain calm, to approach this new lead with the same meticulous care she applied to all aspects of her work.

"Alright, team," she said, straightening up and meeting each of their eyes in turn. "We've got a new angle to pursue. Let's dig deeper into this connection between Robert and John. I want to know everything about their relationship, no matter how small the detail might seem."

As her team sprang into action around her, Sarah allowed herself a small smile. They were one step closer to unraveling the mystery surrounding Evelyn's murder. And she wouldn't rest until justice was served.

Sarah's eyes widened, her piercing gaze fixed on the bank statement before her. The pieces of the puzzle suddenly clicked into place, sending a jolt through her body. She inhaled sharply, her hand trembling slightly as she traced the line showing the transfer of funds.

"This is it," she muttered, more to herself than anyone else. Her mind raced, connecting dots that had seemed unrelated just moments ago. The secret transactions, the timing of Evelyn's murder, Robert's alibi that never quite sat right with her - it all made sense now.

Lifting her head, Sarah locked eyes with her team. "Everyone, gather 'round. We've got something." Her voice was steady, but there was an unmistakable urgency in her tone.

As the team huddled closer, Sarah spread out the bank statement on the table. "Look at this," she said, pointing to the incriminating line. "A transfer of $50,000 from Robert Langdon's account to John Blackwood's, just two days before Evelyn's murder."

Detective Collins leaned in, his brow furrowing. "Holy shit, Sarah. You think this was payment for-"

"The hit?" Sarah finished, her voice grim. "It's looking that way."

Officer Martinez shook her head in disbelief. "I can't believe it. Robert seemed so... normal when we interviewed him."

Sarah's lips tightened into a thin line. "That's often the case with the worst ones," she said, thinking back to cases that had taught her that lesson the hard way. "They're experts at putting on a show."

As the gravity of the situation sank in, a heavy silence fell over the room. Sarah could see the shock and realization mirrored in her team's expressions - the same emotions she'd felt moments ago.

"So what now, boss?" Collins asked, breaking the silence.

Sarah took a deep breath, her mind already formulating their next steps. "Now," she said, her eyes glinting with determination, "we build our case. And we make damn sure Robert Langdon and John Blackwood pay for what they've done."

Sarah's gaze swept across her team, noting their determined expressions. "Alright, let's break this down. What are we thinking about motive?"

Detective Collins scratched his chin. "Well, Robert's the husband. Classic case of wanting to get rid of the wife, maybe?"

Officer Martinez chimed in, her voice tinged with disgust. "And John's the hired muscle. A cold-blooded killer for cash."

Sarah nodded, her mind racing. "Good, but we need more. What about Robert's background? His mother's expectations, his constant struggle with inadequacy..."

"You think that played a role?" Collins asked, eyebrows raised.

Sarah's eyes narrowed. "I do. A man like Robert, always trying to meet impossible standards... Maybe Evelyn became another 'expectation' he couldn't live up to."

The team exchanged glances, the pieces starting to fit together. Sarah could almost feel the energy in the room shift as they honed in on their targets.

"Alright, team," Sarah said, her voice taking on a commanding tone. "I want us to dig deeper into these financial records. Look for any other suspicious transactions, any patterns we might have missed."

She turned to Martinez. "I need you to go through Robert's personal and business accounts with a fine-tooth comb. Look for anything out of the ordinary, no matter how small."

"On it, boss," Martinez replied, already reaching for her laptop.

Sarah's gaze shifted to Collins. "You focus on John's finances. I want to know where every penny of that $50,000 went. And check for any other large deposits he might have received in the past year."

As her team sprang into action, Sarah felt a familiar surge of adrenaline. They were close, she could feel it. And she wouldn't rest until Robert Langdon and John Blackwood faced justice for what they'd done.

Detective Tom Willis leaned back in his chair, his forehead creased with concern. He ran a hand through his salt-and-pepper hair, his eyes fixed on the bank statement in front of him.

"Sarah," he said, his voice tinged with doubt, "I hate to be the devil's advocate here, but are we sure these transactions are enough? I mean, Robert's a wealthy guy. Couldn't he argue this was just a business deal gone south?"

Sarah's piercing gaze locked onto Tom. She felt a flicker of irritation, but pushed it aside. Tom was good at his job, and his cautiousness had saved them from jumping to conclusions before.

"It's a fair question, Tom," she replied, her tone measured. She stood up, pacing the small room as she gathered her thoughts. The faint smell of stale coffee and printer ink filled her nostrils, grounding her in the familiar environment of their makeshift office.

"These transactions aren't just a smoking gun," Sarah continued, her voice gaining conviction with each word. "They're the linchpin that ties everything together." She walked to the evidence board, tapping a photo of Robert Langdon's polished, smiling face.

"We've got Robert's alibi falling apart, thanks to that gas station footage. We have John's suspicious behavior in the days leading up to Evelyn's murder. And now," she emphasized, holding up the bank statement, "we have a clear financial link between them."

Tom nodded slowly, his skepticism visibly wavering. Sarah pressed on, her mind racing through the evidence they'd collected.

"Think about it," she said, a hint of excitement creeping into her voice. "Robert's the kind of man who's spent his entire life trying to meet impossible standards. What if Evelyn became just another expectation he couldn't live up to?"

She paused, letting the idea sink in. The room was silent, save for the soft hum of computers and the distant sound of traffic outside.

"These transactions," Sarah concluded, her eyes sweeping across her team, "they're the final piece of the puzzle. They show motive, they show collaboration, and most importantly, they show premeditation."

A small smile tugged at the corners of her mouth as she saw understanding dawn on her colleagues' faces. "We've got them," she said softly, more to herself than anyone else. "Now we just need to make sure this case is airtight."

Sarah's piercing gaze swept across the room, her mind already mapping out their next steps. "Alright, team, let's divide and conquer," she announced, her voice carrying a mix of determination and urgency.

Detective Tom nodded, his earlier skepticism replaced by renewed focus. "I'll keep digging into these financial records," he offered, gesturing to the stack of papers before him. "There might be more transactions we've missed."

"Good," Sarah replied, her eyes darting to another team member. "Lisa, I want you to focus on Robert and John's known associates. Look for any connections, no matter how small. We need to know if there are other players involved."

Lisa nodded briskly, her fingers already flying across her keyboard. The soft clacking filled the room, a steady rhythm underlying the tension in the air.

Sarah's mind raced, piecing together the implications of their discovery. She paced the length of the makeshift office, her steps quick and purposeful. "We're closing in on them," she muttered, more to herself than the others. "But if we're onto something big..."

She trailed off, a chill running down her spine. Turning abruptly to face her team, Sarah's expression was grave. "We need to move fast," she said, her voice low and urgent. "If Robert and John catch wind of our progress, they might try to cover their tracks or worse, flee."

Detective Rodriguez looked up from his computer, concern etched on his face. "You think they might already know we're onto them?"

Sarah's lips pressed into a thin line. "It's possible. Robert's got connections, and John... well, he's always seemed to have a sixth sense for danger." She couldn't shake the image of John's piercing gaze, as if he could see right through people's intentions.

"What's our timeline looking like?" Lisa asked, her eyes never leaving her screen.

Sarah glanced at her watch, feeling the weight of each passing second. "We need solid evidence linking them both to the murder within the next 48 hours. After that, the risk of them slipping away increases exponentially."

The urgency in her voice seemed to electrify the room. Her team members exchanged determined looks, their movements becoming more focused and deliberate.

As Sarah turned back to her own workstation, her mind wandered to Robert Langdon. She could almost see his charming smile, hiding the turmoil beneath. "What pushed you over the edge, Robert?" she whispered to herself, staring at his photograph. "And how deep does this conspiracy really go?"

Detective Rodriguez pushed his chair back, the wheels squeaking against the linoleum floor. "We can't wait any longer, Sarah. We've got enough to bring them in for questioning at least. Let's make the arrests now before they slip through our fingers."

Lisa's head snapped up, her brow furrowed. "Hold on, Mike. We're close, but we need more concrete evidence. If we move too soon, their lawyers will tear our case apart."

Sarah felt the tension in the room ratchet up a notch. She leaned against the table, her palms pressed flat against its cool surface, as she weighed both arguments in her mind.

"I see merit in both approaches," she began, her voice steady despite the internal conflict. "Mike's right that time is critical. Robert's charm and John's street smarts make them flight risks." She paused, picturing John's wary eyes, always searching for an escape route. "But Lisa has a point about building a rock-solid case."

The team waited, their gazes fixed on Sarah. She could feel the weight of their expectations, reminding her of the pressure Robert must have felt from his mother. She pushed the thought aside, focusing on the decision at hand.

"We'll proceed with caution," Sarah announced, her tone brooking no argument. "We'll intensify our surveillance on both suspects, but we won't move in until we have ironclad evidence linking them directly to Evelyn's murder."

She saw Mike's shoulders slump slightly in disappointment, while Lisa nodded in agreement.

"I know it's a risk," Sarah continued, her voice softening. "But we can't let them slip away, and we can't give them any opportunity to wriggle out of this on a technicality. We owe it to Evelyn to do this right."

The mention of the victim's name seemed to galvanize the team. They nodded in unison, a renewed sense of purpose evident in their expressions.

"Alright, people," Sarah said, clapping her hands together. "Let's get back to work. We've got two days to build an airtight case against Robert Langdon and John Blackwood. Every piece of evidence, every connection, no matter how small—I want it found and verified."

As the team dispersed to their tasks, Sarah's phone buzzed in her pocket. She glanced at the screen, frowning at the unfamiliar number. Normally, she'd let it go to voicemail, but something—intuition, perhaps—made her answer.

"Detective Mitchell," she said, her voice clipped and professional.

"I have information about Evelyn Langdon's murder," a distorted voice crackled through the speaker. "And the secret transactions between Robert and John."

Sarah's eyes widened, her heart rate quickening. She snapped her fingers, gesturing frantically at Lisa to start a trace on the call.

"Who is this?" Sarah asked, fighting to keep her voice steady.

"That's not important," the voice replied. "What matters is what I know."

Sarah's mind raced, analyzing every nuance of the caller's words. "Alright, I'm listening," she said, her tone cautious but encouraging.

"The money transfers, they weren't just about the murder," the caller continued. "There's more to it, a bigger conspiracy. Robert and John, they're just pawns in a larger game."

Sarah's brow furrowed, her free hand clenching into a fist. "What kind of game? Who's behind it?"

There was a pause, and for a heart-stopping moment, Sarah thought the caller had hung up. Then, "It goes back years, Detective. To Evelyn's past. She wasn't who everyone thought she was."

Sarah's eyes widened further, her pulse pounding in her ears. She opened her mouth to ask another question, but the line went dead.

She lowered the phone slowly, her mind reeling. The team gathered around her, their faces a mix of curiosity and concern.

"What was that about?" Mike asked, breaking the tense silence.

Sarah looked at each of them in turn, her expression a blend of shock and determination. "We've been looking at this all wrong," she said quietly. "This isn't just about Robert and John. There's something much bigger at play here."

She paused, taking a deep breath. "And it all leads back to Evelyn Langdon herself."

Chapter 11

You should not include plot points 1 and 2 at the beginning of your response. Instead, begin writing the scene immediately:

The precinct buzzed with frenetic energy as Sarah Mitchell strode through the bullpen, her sharp eyes taking in every detail. Phones rang incessantly, keyboards clacked, and harried officers rushed past with stacks of files clutched to their chests. The air was thick with tension and the acrid smell of stale coffee.

Sarah approached her team, huddled around a whiteboard covered in photos and scrawled notes. Detective Rodriguez looked up, his usually jovial face creased with worry.

"Any progress on the surveillance footage?" Sarah asked, her tone clipped and focused.

Rodriguez shook his head. "Still combing through it. Nothing solid yet."

Sarah nodded, her mind already racing ahead to the next lead. She opened her mouth to speak when her phone buzzed insistently in her pocket. Fishing it out, she glanced at the screen and suppressed a sigh. Chief Parker.

"Mitchell," she answered, bracing herself.

The chief's voice crackled through the speaker, tense and urgent. "Where are we on the Evelyn case? The mayor's breathing down my neck, and the press is having a field day."

Sarah pinched the bridge of her nose, fighting back a wave of frustration. "We're pursuing several leads, sir. My team is working around the clock��"

"That's not good enough, Mitchell," the chief cut in. "We need a breakthrough, and we need it yesterday. This psycho's got the whole city on edge."

Sarah's jaw tightened. *As if I don't know that,* she thought bitterly. *As if I'm not feeling the weight of every passing minute.*

"Understood, sir," she replied, keeping her voice level. "We'll double our efforts."

"See that you do," the chief said gruffly before hanging up.

Sarah lowered the phone, her mind whirling. She knew the pressure was mounting, could feel it pressing down on her shoulders like a physical weight. But she'd be damned if she'd let it compromise her investigation.

"Everything okay, boss?" Rodriguez asked, concern evident in his voice.

Sarah managed a tight smile. "Just the usual song and dance. Come on, let's go over what we've got one more time. There's something we're missing, I can feel it."

As she turned back to the whiteboard, Sarah's determination burned bright and fierce. She'd solve this case, bring Evelyn's killer to justice. No matter what it took.

As Sarah turned away from her team, a flurry of movement caught her eye. A woman with perfectly coiffed hair and a microphone clutched in her manicured hand was weaving through the busy precinct, her gaze locked on Sarah like a heat-seeking missile.

"Detective Mitchell!" the reporter called out, her voice carrying over the din of the station. "Cassandra Lane, Channel 7 News. Can you give us an update on the Evelyn Carter case?"

Sarah's shoulders tensed, but she kept her face neutral. "Ms. Lane, I'm afraid I don't have time for—"

"The public is terrified, Detective," Cassandra pressed, thrusting the microphone closer. "Is there any progress? Any leads?"

Sarah's piercing eyes met the reporter's eager gaze. "We're pursuing all available avenues of investigation," she said firmly, her tone brooking no argument. "Now, if you'll excuse me, I have work to do."

Without waiting for a response, Sarah strode back to her team, her mind already refocusing on the case. She could feel the reporter's disappointed stare boring into her back, but she pushed the guilt aside. There were more important things at stake than sound bites.

"Alright, people," Sarah announced, her voice carrying a note of steely determination. "Let's go over everything again. Rodriguez, what do we have on the forensics?"

As her team gathered around the evidence board, Sarah's keen eyes swept over the photographs, reports, and timelines pinned there. There has to be something we're missing, she thought, her brow furrowing in concentration. Some detail, some connection...

"The DNA results came back inconclusive," Rodriguez reported, frustration evident in his voice. "But we did find traces of an unusual pollen on the victim's clothing."

Sarah's head snapped up. "Pollen? What kind?"

As Rodriguez explained, Sarah's mind raced, piecing together fragments of information. Could this be the breakthrough they needed? Or just another dead end in a case that seemed determined to thwart them at every turn?

Sarah took a deep breath, smoothing down her blazer as she faced the sea of cameras and microphones. The police station steps weren't an ideal backdrop, but they'd have to do. She'd rehearsed this statement in her head a dozen times, carefully weighing each word.

"Good afternoon," she began, her voice steady and authoritative. "I'm Detective Sarah Mitchell, lead investigator on the Evelyn Carter case. At this time, we're actively pursuing several promising leads. While I can't disclose specifics that might compromise our investigation, I want to assure the public that we're working tirelessly to bring the perpetrator to justice."

A barrage of questions erupted, but Sarah held up a hand. "We appreciate your patience and understanding. Anyone with information, no matter how insignificant it may seem, is urged to come forward. Thank you."

As she turned to leave, Sarah caught sight of Evelyn's parents in the crowd, their eyes pleading. It took every ounce of her willpower not to reveal more.

Back inside, Sarah's team was preparing for witness interviews. "Remember," she cautioned, "these people are scared. We need information, but we also need to be sensitive."

Their first interview was with Mrs. Patel, Evelyn's neighbor. The elderly woman's hands trembled as she clutched her teacup.

"Mrs. Patel," Sarah began gently, "can you tell us about the night Evelyn disappeared?"

Mrs. Patel's eyes darted nervously. "I... I don't know anything," she stammered.

Sarah leaned forward, her voice low and reassuring. "Every detail helps, no matter how small. Did you hear or see anything unusual?"

The woman hesitated, then whispered, "There was a car. Idling. I've never seen it before."

As Mrs. Patel described the vehicle, Sarah felt a glimmer of hope. It wasn't much, but it was a start. And in this case, they needed every lead they could get.

Sarah's phone buzzed as she left the interview room. An unknown number. She frowned, answering cautiously. "Detective Mitchell."

A distorted voice crackled through the speaker. "Back off, detective. You're getting too close. Next time, it won't be a warning."

The line went dead. Sarah's heart raced, but she kept her composure, quickly striding to her team.

"Trace that call," she ordered, her voice steady despite the adrenaline coursing through her veins. "And get me everything we have on Evelyn's case. We're not stopping until we crack this."

As night fell, the precinct hummed with activity. Sarah stood before a board covered in photos and notes, her eyes scanning every detail.

"Coffee?" Detective Rodriguez offered, holding out a steaming cup.

Sarah accepted gratefully. "Thanks. Any luck with the phone trace?"

Rodriguez shook his head. "Burner phone. Dead end."

Sarah sighed, rubbing her temples. "Okay, let's go over everything again. There has to be something we're missing."

Hours ticked by. Empty coffee cups littered desks. Sarah paced, muttering to herself, "What are we not seeing?"

Detective Chen yawned. "Maybe we should call it a night, start fresh in the morning?"

Sarah shook her head vehemently. "No. Evelyn deserves justice. We keep going."

As she turned back to the board, Sarah's gaze fell on a seemingly insignificant detail in one of the crime scene photos. Her eyes widened.

"Wait a minute," she breathed. "Look at this. Could it be...?"

The team huddled around, a new energy filling the room. They might just have found their breakthrough.

Sarah slammed her fist on the desk, causing her coffee mug to rattle precariously. The promising lead from the crime scene photo had fizzled out, leaving her more frustrated than ever. She ran her fingers through her disheveled hair, her piercing eyes bloodshot from lack of sleep.

"Damn it!" she muttered, loud enough for nearby officers to glance her way. Sarah barely noticed, her mind racing through the case details for the hundredth time. The weight of Evelyn's unsolved murder pressed down on her shoulders like a physical burden.

Detective Rodriguez approached cautiously. "Sarah, maybe we should—"

"No," she cut him off sharply. "We're not taking a break. We're not giving up." Her voice softened slightly as she added, "Evelyn's family is counting on us."

Sarah's gaze fell on a file folder. Inside was information on their primary suspect, Mark Holloway. Something about his alibi had never sat right with her. She grabbed her jacket.

"I'm going to have another chat with Holloway," she announced, striding towards the door.

"Want backup?" Rodriguez called after her.

Sarah paused, considering. Her instinct was to go alone, but she forced herself to nod. "Meet me there in twenty."

Thirty minutes later, Sarah stood face-to-face with Mark Holloway in his dimly lit living room. His nervous energy was palpable.

"Mr. Holloway," Sarah began, her tone deceptively calm, "I need you to walk me through your whereabouts on the night of May 15th again."

Holloway fidgeted. "I've already told you—"

"Tell me again," Sarah interrupted, her eyes never leaving his face. She noted the slight tremor in his hands, the way his gaze darted to the left.

As Holloway recounted his story, Sarah's mind cataloged every inconsistency, every micro-expression that hinted at deception. She allowed him to finish before pouncing.

"That's interesting, Mr. Holloway," she said, leaning forward slightly. "Because we have new evidence that puts you near Evelyn's apartment that night. Care to explain that?"

It wasn't entirely true, but Sarah watched Holloway's reaction carefully. His face paled, and a bead of sweat formed on his brow.

"I... I don't know what you're talking about," he stammered.

Sarah pressed harder, her voice low and intense. "Don't lie to me, Mark. What really happened that night?"

As she continued to push, Sarah could feel they were on the verge of a breakthrough. But whether it would lead to the truth or another dead end remained to be seen.

Sarah's fingers trembled slightly as she lifted the plastic evidence bag, her keen eyes scrutinizing the contents. Inside lay a tattered business card, its edges frayed and stained with what appeared to be dried blood. The team huddled around her, their breaths held in anticipation.

"This could be it," Sarah murmured, her voice barely above a whisper. She turned to her colleague, Detective Johnson. "Where exactly did you find this?"

Johnson's eyes lit up. "It was wedged between the floorboards in Evelyn's apartment. Must've been overlooked in the initial sweep."

Sarah's mind raced, connecting dots. "The card's for Blackwell Industries. Wasn't that mentioned in one of our witness statements?"

"Yes!" exclaimed Officer Chen, frantically flipping through her notes. "A neighbor mentioned seeing a van with that logo parked outside Evelyn's building the week before her disappearance."

Sarah felt a surge of hope, but quickly tempered it. She'd learned the hard way that leads could fizzle as quickly as they appeared. "Alright, let's not get ahead of ourselves. Johnson, I want you to run a full background check on Blackwell Industries. Chen, see if you can track down that neighbor for a more detailed statement."

As her team dispersed, Sarah's phone buzzed. She glanced at the screen and her heart sank. It was the lab results she'd been waiting for, but not the ones she'd hoped for.

"Damn it," she muttered, rubbing her temples.

"Bad news?" Detective Moore asked, concern etched on his face.

Sarah sighed. "The DNA from the hair we found doesn't match any of our suspects. We're back to square one on that front."

Moore's shoulders slumped, but he quickly straightened up. "We've hit walls before, Sarah. We'll find another way."

Sarah nodded, grateful for his unwavering optimism. "You're right. Let's focus on this new lead. I have a feeling Blackwell Industries might be the key we've been looking for."

As they dove back into their work, Sarah felt the familiar mix of determination and anxiety churning in her gut. The case had thrown countless curveballs their way, but she refused to let it beat her. Evelyn deserved justice, and Sarah was determined to deliver it, no matter how many sleepless nights it took.

Sarah's phone rang, cutting through the bustling noise of the precinct. She glanced at the caller ID and frowned, not recognizing the number.

"Detective Mitchell," she answered, her voice crisp and professional.

"Detective, this is Alison Reed from the Daily Chronicle," came a breathless voice. "I think I've got something you'll want to hear about the Evelyn case."

Sarah's eyes narrowed. Journalists rarely brought good news. "Go on," she said cautiously.

"I've been digging into Blackwell Industries," Alison continued, excitement evident in her tone. "One of their former employees reached out to me. Says he has information about some shady dealings that might be connected to Evelyn's disappearance."

Sarah's heart raced, but she kept her voice steady. "And why is he coming to you instead of the police?"

"He's scared, Detective. But he's willing to talk if you can guarantee his safety."

Sarah's mind whirled with possibilities. This could be the break they needed. "Tell him to come in. We'll protect him."

After hanging up, Sarah quickly assembled her team. "We've got a lead," she announced. "And a search warrant to execute. Let's move."

Twenty minutes later, Sarah stood outside a modest suburban home, her team flanking her. The search warrant felt heavy in her pocket.

"Remember," she said, her piercing gaze sweeping over her colleagues, "we're looking for anything that might connect our suspect to Evelyn or Blackwell Industries. Leave no stone unturned."

As they entered the house, Sarah's keen eyes scanned every surface. The living room was cluttered but unremarkable. She moved methodically, opening drawers and checking behind picture frames.

"Detective!" Officer Chen called from the study. "You need to see this."

Sarah hurried over, her heart pounding. Chen pointed to an open laptop on the desk. On the screen was an email draft addressed to Evelyn.

"My God," Sarah breathed, leaning in to read. "This is it. This is the connection we've been looking for."

As she absorbed the damning contents of the email, Sarah felt a mix of triumph and dread. They were closer than ever to solving the case, but the truth promised to be far more complex and dangerous than they had imagined.

Sarah's eyes darted across the screen, absorbing every word of the incriminating email. Her mind raced, connecting dots and forming new theories. She was so engrossed that she nearly jumped when her phone buzzed in her pocket.

"Mitchell," she answered tersely, her gaze still fixed on the laptop.

"Detective, it's Jameson from forensics," came the rushed voice on the other end. "We've got something big. You need to get back to the station right away."

Sarah's brow furrowed. "What is it? We're in the middle of a crucial search here."

"It's about the DNA evidence from Evelyn's necklace. We ran it through the database again and... well, you're not going to believe this."

Sarah's heart began to race. "Spit it out, Jameson."

"The DNA... it's a partial match to someone in our system. Someone close to the investigation."

Sarah felt the air leave her lungs. "Who?" she demanded, her voice barely above a whisper.

As Jameson spoke the name, Sarah's world tilted on its axis. She gripped the edge of the desk, her knuckles turning white.

"That's... that's impossible," she muttered, her mind reeling.

"I triple-checked, Detective. It's a match."

Sarah ended the call, her hand shaking slightly. She turned to her team, who were watching her with concerned expressions.

"We need to get back to the station. Now." Her voice was steady, but inside, she was in turmoil. Everything they thought they knew about this case had just been turned upside down.

As they left the house, Sarah cast one last glance at the laptop. The pieces were falling into place, but the picture they were forming was far more sinister than she could have ever imagined.

Chapter 12

Sarah's phone vibrated against her hip, slicing through the monotonous hum of the police station. She glanced at the caller ID, her brow furrowing at the unfamiliar number.

"Detective Mitchell," she answered crisply, her free hand absently shuffling case files on her desk.

"Is this Sarah Mitchell?" A trembling voice crackled through the line. "I'm calling about Linda Carter. There's been an incident."

Sarah's blood ran cold, her fingers tightening around the phone. "What kind of incident?" she demanded, already rising from her chair.

"She's been attacked. We found her unconscious in her apartment. She's on her way to Memorial Hospital now."

The world seemed to tilt on its axis. Sarah's heart thundered in her chest as she grabbed her jacket, nearly knocking over her lukewarm coffee in her haste.

"I'm on my way," she barked into the phone, ending the call as she sprinted towards the exit.

Officer Johnson called out as she passed, "Hey Mitchell, where's the fire?"

"Can't talk now," Sarah shouted over her shoulder, bursting through the station doors into the crisp evening air.

Her mind raced as she fumbled with her car keys. Linda. Attacked. How? Why? The questions swirled like a maelstrom as she peeled out of the parking lot, tires screeching.

Sarah weaved through traffic, her siren wailing. "Come on, come on," she muttered, drumming her fingers against the steering wheel at a red light.

An elderly woman in the crosswalk shot her a disapproving look. Any other day, Sarah might have found it amusing. Now, she barely registered it, her thoughts consumed by her friend lying hurt and alone.

As she sped towards the hospital, Sarah's analytical mind kicked into overdrive. Who would want to harm Linda? The woman was a saint, for crying out loud. She volunteered at animal shelters and baked cookies for her neighbors.

"I should have been there," Sarah berated herself, gripping the wheel so tightly her knuckles turned white. "I should have known something was wrong."

But she hadn't known. And now Linda was paying the price for her oversight.

Sarah's jaw clenched as she pulled into the hospital parking lot. Whoever did this would pay. She'd make damn sure of that.

Sarah burst through the hospital's sliding doors, the antiseptic smell assaulting her senses. The bustling emergency room was a cacophony of beeping machines, hurried footsteps, and urgent voices. Her keen eyes darted around, taking in every detail as she approached the nurse's station.

"Linda Carter," Sarah said, her voice steady despite her racing heart. "Where is she?"

The nurse barely glanced up from her computer. "Are you family?"

Sarah's fingers drummed impatiently on the counter. "I'm Detective Sarah Mitchell. Linda's my—" she hesitated, then continued, "She's a witness in an ongoing investigation."

"Third floor, room 312," the nurse replied, eyeing Sarah's badge.

As Sarah strode towards the elevators, her mind whirled. What if Linda's condition was worse than she'd been told? What if—

"Hold the door!" A doctor called out, rushing towards her.

Sarah's hand shot out, catching the elevator door. As they ascended, she found herself studying the doctor's face, searching for any sign of concern or urgency that might relate to Linda.

"Rough night?" the doctor asked, noticing her intense stare.

Sarah blinked, realizing how she must look. "You could say that," she muttered, relieved when the elevator dinged for the third floor.

She navigated the maze-like corridors, her footsteps echoing in the quiet hallway. Room 312 loomed ahead, and Sarah paused, taking a deep breath to steel herself.

Pushing the door open, Sarah's eyes immediately found Linda. Her friend lay still in the hospital bed, her usually vibrant face marred by bruises and cuts. Bandages wrapped around her head and left arm. The steady beep of the heart monitor filled the room.

"Oh, Linda," Sarah whispered, her professional demeanor cracking for a moment. She moved to the bedside, carefully taking Linda's uninjured hand in hers.

Linda's eyes fluttered open, a weak smile spreading across her battered face. "Sarah," she croaked, "you came."

"Of course I came," Sarah replied, her voice thick with emotion. "How are you feeling?"

"Like I picked a fight with a freight train," Linda joked weakly, wincing as she tried to shift in the bed.

Sarah's lips twitched in a brief smile. Even now, Linda was trying to lighten the mood. "Do you remember what happened?" she asked gently, her detective instincts kicking in despite her concern.

Linda's brow furrowed. "It's... fuzzy. I was leaving work late, and then..." She trailed off, her eyes growing distant.

"It's okay," Sarah reassured her, squeezing her hand. "We'll figure this out. I promise."

As Linda drifted back to sleep, Sarah's jaw set with determination. Whoever did this would face justice. She'd make sure of it, even if she had to work around the clock to find them.

Sarah's thumb traced small circles on Linda's hand as she sat by the bed, her mind a whirlwind of emotions. Anger simmered beneath her composed exterior, mingling with a fierce protectiveness for her friend. She blinked rapidly, fighting back the sting of tears.

"I'll find who did this to you, Linda," Sarah whispered, her voice barely audible over the rhythmic beeping of the monitors. "I swear it."

A gentle knock on the door frame interrupted her thoughts. Sarah looked up to see a man in a crisp suit standing in the doorway, his badge glinting under the harsh hospital lights.

"Detective Mitchell?" he asked, stepping into the room. "I'm Detective Jake Reeves, assigned to Ms. Carter's case."

Sarah stood, her professional mask sliding back into place. "Nice to meet you, Detective Reeves. What can you tell me about the attack?"

Reeves glanced at Linda's sleeping form before answering. "Not much yet, I'm afraid. The attack occurred around 9:30 PM in the parking lot of the community center where Ms. Carter works. No witnesses have come forward so far."

Sarah's brow furrowed. "Any surveillance footage?"

"We're working on obtaining it," Reeves replied. "The cameras in that area have been on the fritz lately. Typical budget cuts," he added with a grimace.

Sarah's mind raced, cataloging potential leads and avenues of investigation. "What about physical evidence?" she pressed.

Reeves sighed. "Some blood spatter, possibly from the attacker. We're running it now, but..."

"But it'll take time," Sarah finished, frustration evident in her voice. She glanced back at Linda, her resolve strengthening. "Keep me in the loop, Detective. I want to help however I can."

"Of course," Reeves nodded. "We'll find who did this, Mitchell. Two heads are better than one."

As Reeves left, Sarah settled back into her chair, her keen eyes sweeping over Linda's injuries. She may not be officially on the case, but that wouldn't stop her from pursuing every lead. For Linda's sake, she'd leave no stone unturned.

Sarah's fingers twitched with restless energy as she strode out of the hospital, her mind already piecing together a plan of action. The crisp night air hit her face, a welcome jolt after hours in the sterile hospital environment.

"Time to get to work," she muttered, fishing her car keys from her pocket.

As she drove towards the community center, Sarah's thoughts raced. She'd known Linda for years - who would want to hurt her? And why? The questions gnawed at her, fueling her determination.

Pulling up to the crime scene, Sarah's breath caught in her throat. Yellow police tape fluttered in the breeze, cordoning off a large section of the parking lot. Even in the dim streetlights, dark stains marred the asphalt - Linda's blood.

"Christ," Sarah whispered, stepping out of her car. The violence of the attack was palpable, hanging in the air like a suffocating fog.

As she approached, a young officer moved to intercept her. "Ma'am, this is an active crime scene-"

Sarah flashed her badge. "Detective Mitchell. I'm assisting with the investigation."

The officer's eyes widened slightly. "Oh, of course. Sorry, Detective."

Sarah nodded, her gaze already sweeping the area. "What can you tell me about the scene?"

The officer shifted nervously. "It's... pretty bad, ma'am. The victim was found there," he pointed to a spot near a dumpster, "badly beaten. We think she was ambushed as she was leaving work."

Sarah's jaw clenched. "Any signs of robbery?"

"No, ma'am. Her purse was still with her, untouched."

Sarah's brow furrowed. Not a random mugging, then. This was personal. She crouched near the bloodstains, her keen eyes searching for anything the techs might have missed.

"Has the neighborhood been canvassed?" she asked, not looking up.

"Yes, ma'am. But..." the officer hesitated.

Sarah glanced at him sharply. "But what?"

He swallowed hard. "People seem... scared. More than usual for this kind of thing."

Sarah stood, her expression grim. "Fear can make people clam up. Or it can make them talk." She pulled out her notebook. "I'll need a list of everyone interviewed so far."

As the officer hurried to comply, Sarah turned back to the scene, her resolve hardening. Someone out there knew something, and she was going to find out what. For Linda's sake, and for the sake of a neighborhood now gripped by terror.

Sarah approached the first house on her list, a modest bungalow with peeling paint and overgrown shrubs. She rapped sharply on the door, her eyes scanning the street as she waited. After a moment, the door cracked open, revealing a wary face.

"Mrs. Hernandez?" Sarah asked, flashing her badge. "I'm Detective Mitchell. I'd like to ask you a few questions about what happened last night."

The woman's eyes darted nervously. "I already talked to the police."

Sarah nodded, her tone softening. "I know, and I appreciate that. But sometimes details come back to us later. Anything you remember, no matter how small, could be crucial."

Mrs. Hernandez hesitated, then opened the door wider. "I suppose I could spare a few minutes."

As they settled in the living room, Sarah noticed the woman's trembling hands. "Did you hear or see anything unusual last night?" she asked gently.

Mrs. Hernandez shook her head. "No, nothing. I was watching TV and..."

Sarah leaned forward, her piercing gaze locked on the woman. "But?"

"Well," Mrs. Hernandez whispered, "there was a car. It's been parked down the street for days. I thought it was odd."

Sarah's pulse quickened. "Can you describe it?"

As Mrs. Hernandez spoke, Sarah jotted notes, her mind racing. This could be the break they needed. But as she pressed for more details, she sensed the woman's growing unease.

"I'm not sure I should say more," Mrs. Hernandez muttered, wringing her hands. "What if they come after me next?"

Sarah felt a surge of frustration, but kept her voice calm. "I understand your concern, but your information could help prevent another attack. We can protect you."

Mrs. Hernandez shook her head vehemently. "No, I'm sorry. I can't risk it. Please, you should go now."

As the door closed behind her, Sarah clenched her fists. One step forward, two steps back. But she couldn't give up. Linda was counting on her, and so was this terrified neighborhood.

Sarah took a deep breath, steadying herself. She turned back to Mrs. Hernandez's door and knocked again, her knuckles rapping with quiet determination.

"Mrs. Hernandez, please," Sarah called through the door, her voice gentle but firm. "I know you're scared, but I promise you, we can keep you safe."

The door cracked open, just an inch. Sarah could see one of Mrs. Hernandez's worried eyes peering out.

"How?" the woman whispered.

Sarah's mind raced, weighing her options. "We can arrange for increased patrols in your area, and I can personally check in on you regularly. Your statement can be anonymous in our reports."

Mrs. Hernandez hesitated, then slowly opened the door wider. Sarah offered a reassuring smile, though her heart was pounding.

"Your cooperation could save lives," Sarah continued, her voice low and earnest. "Every detail helps us build a clearer picture. Together, we can stop this person before they hurt anyone else."

As Mrs. Hernandez nodded hesitantly, Sarah's phone buzzed. She glanced down to see a message from the forensics team. They were ready for her at the crime scene.

"Thank you," Sarah said warmly to Mrs. Hernandez. "I'll be in touch soon. Remember, you're doing the right thing."

As she hurried to her car, Sarah's mind was already shifting gears. What would the forensics team have found? She hoped it would be the breakthrough they desperately needed.

Arriving at the cordoned-off area, Sarah ducked under the yellow tape. The lead forensic expert, Dr. Chen, waved her over.

"Detective Mitchell," he greeted her, his gloved hands carefully holding an evidence bag. "We've got some interesting finds."

Sarah peered at the bag's contents. "Fingerprints?"

"Better," Dr. Chen replied with a hint of excitement. "We found traces of DNA on the doorknob. It doesn't match the victim's profile."

Sarah's heart leapt. This could be the key to cracking the case wide open. As she watched the team meticulously combing the area, she felt a glimmer of hope. They were one step closer to bringing Linda's attacker to justice.

The fluorescent lights of the police station buzzed overhead as Sarah hunched over her desk, her eyes bloodshot from hours of staring at the computer screen. The clock on the wall read 2:37 AM, but time had lost all meaning. She rubbed her temples, willing her tired mind to focus on the database in front of her.

"Come on," she muttered, scrolling through another set of potential matches. "There has to be something here."

Her fingers flew across the keyboard, cross-referencing the DNA evidence from Linda's case with every criminal record in the system. Each dead end only fueled her determination.

"Still here, Mitchell?" Detective Rodriguez's voice startled her.

Sarah looked up, blinking away the fatigue. "Yeah, I can't let this go. Linda's attacker is out there, and I won't rest until we find them."

Rodriguez nodded, understanding in his eyes. "Just don't burn yourself out. You're no good to Linda if you're running on fumes."

Sarah managed a weak smile. "I know. I just... I can't shake the feeling that the answer is right here, just out of reach."

As Rodriguez left, Sarah's phone rang. It was Linda's sister, Mary.

"Hi Mary," Sarah answered, her voice softening. "How are you holding up?"

"It's been tough," Mary's voice cracked. "Mom's a wreck, and Dad... he's trying to be strong, but I can see how much this is tearing him apart."

Sarah's heart ached. "I can only imagine. Listen, I promise you, we're doing everything we can to find who did this."

"I know, Sarah. It's just..." Mary hesitated. "Linda had been acting strange lately. Jumpy. Like she was hiding something."

Sarah sat up straighter, her fatigue momentarily forgotten. "Really? Did she mention anything specific?"

"No, but... there was this guy. I saw him hanging around her apartment a few times. Linda brushed it off, said he was just a neighbor, but something felt off."

Sarah's mind raced. This could be the lead they needed. "Mary, that's incredibly helpful. Can you describe him?"

As Mary detailed the mysterious man, Sarah furiously took notes. It wasn't much, but it was a start. A new thread to follow in the tangled web of this case.

"Thank you, Mary. This could really help us," Sarah said, genuine gratitude in her voice. "And please, if you need anything - day or night - don't hesitate to call."

After hanging up, Sarah stared at her notes. The pieces were slowly coming together. With renewed energy, she dove back into her research, determined to connect the dots and bring Linda's attacker to justice.

Sarah's phone buzzed, jolting her from her intense focus. Her heart raced as she saw the hospital's number flash on the screen.

"Detective Mitchell," she answered, her voice tight with anticipation.

"Ms. Mitchell, it's Nurse Chen from County General. I thought you'd want to know - Linda Carter is showing signs of improvement. She's still unconscious, but her vitals are stabilizing."

Sarah exhaled, a wave of relief washing over her. "That's... that's wonderful news. Thank you for letting me know."

As she hung up, Sarah allowed herself a small smile. It wasn't much, but it was something. A glimmer of hope in the darkness that had enveloped them all.

Her moment of respite was short-lived as her phone rang again. An unknown number.

"Detective Mitchell," she answered, her tone cautious.

"Is this the detective working Linda Carter's case?" a trembling voice asked.

Sarah's instincts kicked in. "Yes, it is. Who am I speaking with?"

"I... I don't want to give my name. But I saw something the night Linda was attacked. I've been scared to come forward, but I can't sleep knowing I haven't said anything."

Sarah's heart pounded. This could be it. "I understand your fear, but anything you can tell me could be crucial. Can you describe what you saw?"

The witness hesitated, then began to speak. As Sarah listened, her eyes widened. This wasn't just a lead - it was a potential breakthrough.

"Thank you," she said softly when the caller finished. "You've been incredibly brave. I promise you, we'll do everything we can to keep you safe."

As she hung up, Sarah felt a surge of energy. She had a description, a potential motive, and a timeline that finally made sense. It wasn't everything, but it was enough to reignite her determination.

"I'm coming for you," she whispered to the empty room, her voice filled with quiet intensity. "And I won't stop until I find you."

Chapter 13

Sarah Mitchell leaned forward in her chair, her piercing eyes scanning the evidence board before her. Photos of victims, suspects, and crime scenes stared back at her, connected by a web of red string and hastily scribbled notes. The fluorescent lights of the police station hummed overhead, casting a harsh glow on the gruesome images.

Tap. Tap. Tap.

Her pen drummed an erratic rhythm against the desk, betraying the turmoil beneath her composed exterior. Sarah's mind raced, trying to piece together the puzzle laid out before her.

"There has to be something I'm missing," she muttered, running a hand through her hair. "Some connection I'm not seeing."

She stood up abruptly, the legs of her chair scraping against the linoleum floor. Pacing back and forth, Sarah's gaze never left the board. Her colleagues had long since gone home, leaving her alone with her thoughts and the weight of unsolved cases.

"Okay, Mitchell," she said to herself, her voice barely above a whisper. "Think. What would you tell a rookie to look for?"

Sarah approached the board, her fingers tracing the red string connecting two photos. A flicker of an idea sparked in her mind, but it slipped away before she could grasp it fully.

Frustrated, she returned to her desk, collapsing into her chair with a sigh. The pen found its way back to her hand, resuming its nervous dance against the desktop.

Tap. Tap. Tap.

"Come on, Sarah," she urged herself. "You've cracked tougher cases than this. What are you missing?"

As the night wore on, Sarah remained at her desk, her determined gaze fixed on the evidence board, refusing to give up until she found the breakthrough she knew was waiting just beyond her reach.

The shrill ring of Sarah's phone cut through the silence, startling her. She snatched it up, her voice crisp and professional. "Detective Mitchell."

A distorted voice crackled through the speaker. "Back off the case, Detective. Or you and your team will face consequences you can't imagine."

Sarah's breath caught in her throat, her knuckles whitening as she gripped the phone tighter. "Who is this?" she demanded, her tone sharp.

The line went dead.

Sarah stared at the phone, her heart racing. She took a deep breath, steadying herself. Without hesitation, she dialed Kevin's number.

"Kevin, it's Sarah. I need you and Linda in the office. Now."

Within minutes, Kevin burst through the door, Linda close behind. Sarah's piercing gaze met theirs as they entered.

"What's going on, Sarah?" Linda asked, her warm brown eyes filled with concern.

Sarah's jaw clenched. "We've been threatened. Someone wants us off this case."

Kevin's youthful enthusiasm dampened, replaced by a mix of worry and determination. "What do we do?"

"We stay vigilant," Sarah said, her voice steady despite the fear churning in her stomach. "Double-check everything, trust no one outside this room. Kevin, I need you to trace that call. Linda, review our security protocols."

As they nodded, Sarah's thoughts raced. Who could be behind this? What had they uncovered that was worth threatening them over? She pushed the questions aside, focusing on the task at hand.

"We're close to something big," she said, her eyes scanning the evidence board. "That's why they're scared. We can't back down now."

Linda placed a reassuring hand on Sarah's shoulder. "We're with you, Sarah. All the way."

Sarah nodded, grateful for their support but acutely aware of the danger she'd brought upon them. She couldn't shake the feeling that this case was about to take a dark turn.

Sarah stepped out of her office, her senses on high alert. The familiar hum of the police station now felt ominous, every sound amplified in her heightened state of awareness. The fluorescent lights above flickered erratically, casting dancing shadows across the worn linoleum floor. Each step she took echoed loudly, the creaking of old floorboards beneath her feet sending shivers down her spine.

As she rounded the corner, Sarah caught sight of Detective Johnson's office. She hesitated, her hand hovering over the doorknob. Taking a deep breath, she knocked softly.

"Come in," Johnson's gruff voice called out.

Sarah entered, closing the door behind her. "Got a minute, sir?"

Johnson looked up from his paperwork, his weathered face creasing with concern. "Of course, Mitchell. What's on your mind?"

Sarah sank into the chair across from him, her shoulders slumping. "I... I'm not sure I'm cut out for this case anymore," she admitted, her voice barely above a whisper.

"What makes you say that?" Johnson leaned forward, his eyes searching hers.

"The threats, the pressure... I'm putting my team at risk," Sarah said, fidgeting with her sleeve. "What if I'm not good enough to solve this? What if someone gets hurt because of my mistakes?"

Johnson's expression softened. "Sarah, listen to me. You're one of the best detectives I've ever worked with. Your instincts are sharp, and your dedication is unmatched."

"But what if-"

"No 'what ifs,'" Johnson interrupted gently. "This job isn't about being perfect. It's about perseverance, about getting back up when you're knocked down. And that's exactly what you're doing right now."

Sarah nodded slowly, feeling a small spark of confidence reignite within her. "You really think I can crack this case?"

Johnson smiled, a rare sight that crinkled the corners of his eyes. "I don't think, Mitchell. I know."

Sarah left Johnson's office with renewed determination, her steps purposeful as she headed back to her desk. However, as she approached, she noticed Officer Chen rifling through her files, a look of panic on his face.

"Chen? What's going on?" Sarah asked, her voice sharp with sudden concern.

Chen jumped, nearly dropping the stack of papers in his hands. "Detective Mitchell! I... I'm so sorry. The witness statement from Mrs. Gonzalez – I can't find it anywhere. I've looked through everything twice."

Sarah felt her stomach drop. "What? That's impossible. I put it right here in this folder." She snatched the file from Chen's hands, frantically flipping through the pages. Her heart raced as the reality sank in – the crucial testimony was indeed missing.

"I don't understand," Sarah muttered, more to herself than to Chen. "This can't be happening."

Chen shifted uncomfortably. "Should I inform Detective Johnson?"

"No," Sarah said quickly, her mind already racing. "No, I'll handle this. Thank you, Chen. You can go."

As Chen retreated, Sarah sank into her chair, her earlier boost of confidence evaporating. She closed her eyes, taking a deep breath. "Get it together, Mitchell," she whispered to herself.

Opening her eyes, Sarah pulled the case files closer, spreading them across her desk. "Alright, if that statement's gone, there has to be something else we're missing," she said aloud, her voice tinged with determination.

For hours, Sarah pored over every document, every photograph, every scrap of evidence. Her coffee grew cold, forgotten beside her as she scribbled notes, drew connections, and muttered theories under her breath.

"Come on, come on," she urged, squinting at a grainy surveillance photo. "There's got to be something here."

As the station grew quiet around her, Sarah remained, her dedication unwavering. She was determined to find the overlooked clue that would break the case wide open, proving to herself and everyone else – that she was still the detective they could count on.

Sarah's eyes snapped to the package that had just been placed on her desk. The delivery person was already halfway out the door when she called out, "Wait! Who—"

But they were gone.

Her heart quickened as she eyed the plain brown parcel. No return address. Just her name scrawled in jagged letters.

With trembling hands, Sarah reached for her letter opener. The paper tore easily, revealing a single sheet of paper inside. As she unfolded it, her breath caught in her throat.

"BACK OFF OR ELSE," the message read in cut-out magazine letters.

Sarah's pulse pounded in her ears. She glanced around the nearly empty station, suddenly hyper-aware of every shadow.

"Damn it," she muttered, stuffing the note into her pocket. She needed to think, to process this latest threat.

Before she knew it, Sarah found herself outside Dr. Shaw's office. She hesitated, then knocked.

"Come in," Dr. Shaw's calm voice called.

Sarah entered, closing the door behind her. "I hope I'm not interrupting."

Dr. Shaw smiled warmly. "Not at all, Detective. What's troubling you?"

Sarah sank into a chair, exhaling heavily. "I just... I received a threat. And with everything else going on, I'm starting to wonder if I'm in over my head."

Dr. Shaw leaned forward, her eyes kind but penetrating. "Sarah, tell me. What's really frightening you about this case?"

Sarah's gaze dropped to her hands. "I'm afraid I'll fail. That I'll let everyone down. That I'm not good enough to solve this."

"And why do you believe that?" Dr. Shaw pressed gently.

Sarah looked up, her eyes glistening. "Because I've been wrong before. And people got hurt."

Dr. Shaw nodded slowly. "Sarah, your past experiences have shaped you, but they don't define your capabilities. Your dedication, your attention to detail, these are your strengths. Trust in them."

Sarah felt a small spark of hope ignite within her. "You really think I can do this?"

"I know you can," Dr. Shaw said firmly. "But you need to believe it too."

Sarah left Dr. Shaw's office feeling slightly more grounded, but the weight of responsibility still pressed heavily on her shoulders. She made her way to the break room, where she found her trusted colleague, Detective Kevin Barnes, pouring himself a cup of coffee.

"Hey, Kev," Sarah said, her voice low. "Got a minute?"

Kevin looked up, concern etching his features as he took in Sarah's troubled expression. "Of course. What's up?"

Sarah glanced around, ensuring they were alone before speaking. "I'm worried, Kevin. This case... it's not just about solving a crime anymore. We're all in danger."

Kevin set down his mug, giving Sarah his full attention. "What do you mean?"

Sarah's fingers tapped nervously against her thigh as she spoke. "I received a threat today. Anonymous. They want us to back off the case."

"Jesus, Sarah," Kevin breathed. "Have you told the Captain?"

She shook her head. "Not yet. I... I'm not sure how to handle this. I can't help but think about Linda, about you. What if something happens to either of you because of me?"

Kevin's brow furrowed. "Hey, we're in this together. We knew the risks when we signed up for this job."

Sarah's eyes met his, vulnerability clear in her gaze. "But what if I'm not good enough to crack this case? What if I'm leading us all into danger for nothing?"

Kevin placed a reassuring hand on her shoulder. "Sarah, you're the best detective I know. If anyone can solve this, it's you."

As they stood there, the quiet hum of the break room was suddenly interrupted by Sarah's phone buzzing. She pulled it out, her eyes widening as she read the message.

"Kevin," she breathed, a hint of excitement creeping into her voice. "Remember that partial fingerprint we couldn't place? The lab just got a match. It belongs to a known associate of our prime suspect."

Kevin's face broke into a grin. "That's fantastic! See? I told you we'd get a break."

For the first time in days, Sarah felt a genuine smile tugging at her lips. "You're right. This could be the lead we've been waiting for."

As they hurried out of the break room, Sarah felt a renewed sense of purpose coursing through her veins. The case was far from over, but this breakthrough had reignited her determination. Whatever challenges lay ahead, she was ready to face them head-on.

Chapter 14

Sarah stared out the precinct window, her eyes tracing the city skyline as her mind raced. Linda's recovery had lit a fire within her, rekindling the determination that had begun to flicker in the face of dead ends and false leads. She took a deep breath, feeling the weight of responsibility settle on her shoulders like a familiar coat.

"We're going to crack this case," she murmured to herself, her voice barely audible above the hum of the office. "For Linda. For justice."

A gentle knock on her office door broke Sarah from her reverie. She turned to see Linda standing in the doorway, a warm smile lighting up her face.

"Hey there, Detective Extraordinaire," Linda said, her voice filled with warmth. "Got a minute for an old friend?"

Sarah's lips quirked into a small smile. "For you? Always. Come on in."

Linda settled into the chair across from Sarah's desk, her auburn hair catching the late afternoon sunlight. "How are you holding up? And don't give me that 'I'm fine' routine. I know you better than that."

Sarah sighed, her fingers drumming against the worn surface of her desk. "I'm... determined. Your recovery, Linda, it's given me new hope. New purpose. We're going to solve this, no matter what it takes."

Linda reached across the desk, her hand covering Sarah's restless fingers. "I know you will. And I want you to know how grateful I am, Sarah. Not just for me, but for everyone you're fighting for."

Sarah's eyes met Linda's, seeing the sincerity shining in her friend's warm brown gaze. "I'm just doing my job," she said, her voice gruff with emotion.

Linda shook her head, a gentle laugh escaping her. "Oh, Sarah. Always so modest. You're doing so much more than that, and you know it. We're all in this together, you know. The whole team is behind you, one hundred percent."

Sarah felt a warmth bloom in her chest, battling against her usual cautious nature. "I appreciate that, Linda. More than you know. But this case... it's complicated. Dangerous. I can't help but worry about what might happen if we miss something, if we make a wrong move."

"That's why you're the perfect person to lead this investigation," Linda said, her voice filled with unwavering confidence. "Your attention to detail, your analytical mind – they're your superpowers, Sarah. And combined with the skills of your team? You're unstoppable."

Sarah couldn't help but smile at Linda's enthusiasm. "Your optimism is contagious, you know that?"

Linda grinned, her eyes twinkling. "Good! Someone needs to balance out all that brooding detective energy you've got going on."

As they shared a laugh, Sarah felt some of the tension leave her body. Linda's unwavering support and bright outlook were like a balm to her worried soul. She knew the road ahead would be challenging, but with friends like Linda by her side, Sarah felt ready to face whatever came their way.

Sarah strode into the conference room, her eyes scanning the faces of her team gathered around the table. The air was thick with anticipation and the faint aroma of coffee.

"Alright, everyone," she said, her voice steady and authoritative. "Let's get started. We've got a lot of ground to cover."

As Sarah took her seat at the head of the table, she couldn't help but notice the determined set of each team member's jaw. They were ready for this, just as she was.

"First things first," Sarah began, her gaze sweeping across the room. "I want to hear what each of you has uncovered so far. No detail is too small."

Detective Rodriguez leaned forward, his brow furrowed. "I've been digging into the victim's financials. There's something off about his last few transactions. Large sums of money moving in and out of offshore accounts."

Sarah's mind raced with possibilities. "Good work, Rodriguez. That could be our link to a motive. What else?"

As each team member shared their findings, Sarah felt a familiar thrill. This was where she thrived – piecing together the puzzle, connecting the dots that others might miss.

"What about the neighbor's alibi?" Sarah asked, her piercing gaze landing on Officer Chen.

Chen shook her head. "It doesn't hold up. I checked with the store he claimed to be at during the time of the murder. Their security footage shows no sign of him."

Sarah nodded, her mind already formulating a plan. "Alright, we need to bring him in for questioning. Chen, set that up for this afternoon."

As the meeting progressed, Sarah guided the discussion with a steady hand, drawing out ideas and encouraging collaboration. She could feel the energy in the room building, the collective determination to crack this case growing stronger with each passing minute.

"Remember," Sarah said as the meeting drew to a close, "we're stronger together. Every piece of information, every hunch – share it. This is how we'll solve this case."

As the team filed out, Sarah's mind was already racing ahead to their next move. The neighbor's inconsistent alibi nagged at her. She knew it was time to apply some pressure.

Hours later, Sarah sat across from the neighbor, Mr. Thompson, in the interrogation room. His nervous fidgeting didn't escape her notice.

"Mr. Thompson," Sarah began, her voice calm but firm. "Can you walk me through your whereabouts on the night of July 15th?"

Thompson swallowed hard. "I-I told the other officer. I was at the convenience store on 5th Street."

Sarah leaned forward slightly, her eyes never leaving Thompson's face. "That's interesting, because we've reviewed the store's security footage. You weren't there, Mr. Thompson."

She watched as a bead of sweat formed on his forehead. Got you, she thought.

"Want to try again?" Sarah asked, her tone deceptively casual. "Where were you really that night?"

As Thompson stumbled through a new version of events, Sarah's mind raced, cataloging every inconsistency, every nervous tic. She knew they were getting closer to the truth. The thrill of the chase surged through her veins, tempered by the weight of responsibility she carried.

This is it, Sarah thought. We're on the right track. Now to unravel the rest of this tangled web.

Sarah's eyes flicked to the two-way mirror, knowing Robert and Dr. Shaw were observing the interrogation. She turned back to Mr. Thompson, who was now visibly sweating.

"Let's take a break," Sarah said, standing up. "I'll be right back."

She stepped out of the interrogation room, her mind buzzing. In the adjacent observation room, Robert and Dr. Shaw were hunched over a laptop.

"What've we got?" Sarah asked, peering over their shoulders.

Robert's fingers flew across the keyboard. "I've been cross-referencing Thompson's new story with our surveillance footage. Look at this."

He pulled up a grainy video showing a figure skulking near the victim's house. The timestamp matched Thompson's revised alibi.

"It could be him," Sarah murmured, leaning in closer. "But it's not clear enough for a positive ID."

Dr. Shaw spoke up, her voice thoughtful. "His body language during the interview was extremely telling. The way he gripped the arms of the chair when you mentioned the convenience store – classic defensive posture."

Sarah nodded, feeling a familiar surge of adrenaline. "We're close. I can feel it."

She turned to leave, then paused. "Robert, can you enhance that footage? And Dr. Shaw, I'd like your full psychological assessment when we're done here."

Back in the interrogation room, Sarah settled into her chair, studying Thompson's nervous face. Time to turn up the heat, she thought.

"Mr. Thompson," she began, her voice deceptively calm, "let's talk about your relationship with the victim."

Sarah's eyes narrowed as Thompson shifted uncomfortably in his seat. She was about to press further when Linda burst into the room, her usually calm demeanor replaced by urgency.

"Sarah, we've got a problem," Linda said, her voice low and tense.

Sarah excused herself and followed Linda into the hallway. "What's going on?"

Linda's warm brown eyes were filled with concern. "The convenience store's security footage from the night of the murder? It's gone. Completely wiped."

Sarah felt a knot forming in her stomach. "What? How is that possible?"

"We don't know," Linda replied, running a hand through her auburn hair. "But it gets worse. The store owner claims he was threatened by someone matching Thompson's description. He's refusing to cooperate now."

Sarah leaned against the wall, her mind racing. This was a major setback. The footage could have confirmed or disproved Thompson's alibi. Without it, they were back to square one.

"Alright," Sarah said, taking a deep breath. "We need to regroup. Get everyone in the conference room in ten minutes."

As Linda hurried off, Sarah's analytical mind kicked into overdrive. They needed a new approach, and fast.

In the conference room, the team gathered around the table, tension palpable in the air. Robert's usual confidence seemed shaken, while Dr. Shaw's eyes darted between team members, assessing their reactions.

Sarah stood at the head of the table, her voice steady despite her inner turmoil. "We've hit a roadblock, but we're not giving up. Ideas, people. What do we have left?"

Robert cleared his throat. "We could try reconstructing the timeline using traffic cam footage from surrounding areas. It's a long shot, but..."

"Do it," Sarah nodded. "Linda, I need you to work your magic with the store owner. See if you can get him to open up."

Linda's gentle smile returned. "I'll do my best, Sarah. Maybe a softer approach will help him feel safe enough to talk."

As the team dispersed to their tasks, Sarah felt a glimmer of hope. They were down, but not out. She turned to Dr. Shaw, who had remained quiet throughout the meeting.

"Doctor, I need your insight. What are we missing?"

Dr. Shaw's eyes lit up. "Well, Sarah, I've been analyzing Thompson's body language and speech patterns. There's something off about his alibi, beyond just the missing footage. I think we need to look closer at his personal relationships, especially with the victim."

Sarah nodded, feeling a surge of excitement. "That's it. We've been so focused on the physical evidence, we've neglected the human element. Let's dig deeper into their connection."

As she headed back to the interrogation room, Sarah felt the familiar rush of adrenaline. They might have just found the breakthrough they needed.

Sarah's eyes darted across the evidence board, her mind racing as she connected threads that had previously seemed unrelated. She turned to face her team, who were gathered around the conference table, their expressions a mix of anticipation and exhaustion.

"Alright, listen up," Sarah began, her voice firm but tinged with excitement. "I think I've got something here. We've been looking at this all wrong."

Detective Johnson leaned forward. "What are you thinking, Sarah?"

Sarah grabbed a marker and started sketching on the whiteboard. "The victim's schedule, the missing security footage, Thompson's alibi – they're all connected, but not how we thought."

As she explained her theory, the room came alive with discussion. Linda chimed in, "That would explain the discrepancies in the witness statements!"

"Exactly," Sarah nodded, her piercing eyes scanning the room. "But we need more. Johnson, what about those financial records you were digging into?"

Johnson shuffled through some papers. "Well, there was an unusual transaction the day before the murder. Could be nothing, but..."

"Or it could be everything," Sarah finished. She felt the familiar thrill of pieces falling into place. "Alright, team. We need to move on this now. Thompson's our guy, I'm sure of it."

Within the hour, Sarah found herself outside Thompson's residence, her team positioned strategically around the property. Her heart raced, but her exterior remained calm and focused.

"Remember," she spoke into her radio, "Thompson's smart and potentially dangerous. Stay alert."

As they approached the front door, Sarah's mind raced through possible scenarios. Would he run? Fight? Confess? She took a deep breath, steadying herself.

"Mr. Thompson," she called out, knocking firmly. "This is Detective Mitchell. We need to speak with you."

Silence. Then, the sound of hurried footsteps from inside.

"He's running!" Sarah shouted, adrenaline surging through her veins. "Johnson, cover the back!"

In a fluid motion, Sarah kicked down the door, her gun drawn. The chase was on, and she was determined to end this case once and for all.

Sarah's boots pounded against the hardwood floor as she pursued Thompson through the house. Her breath came in sharp bursts, but her focus remained razor-sharp. As she rounded a corner into the kitchen, doubt suddenly gripped her chest.

"What if we're wrong?" The thought flashed through her mind, causing her to hesitate for a split second. "What if we've missed something crucial?"

She shook her head, pushing the doubt aside. Now wasn't the time for second-guessing. She spotted Thompson disappearing through the back door and sprinted after him.

"Stop! Police!" Sarah shouted, bursting into the backyard. Her eyes darted around, searching for movement.

A rustle from behind a large oak tree caught her attention. Sarah approached cautiously, gun raised.

"It's over, Thompson," she called out, her voice steady despite the hammering of her heart. "Come out slowly with your hands where I can see them."

As Thompson emerged, hands raised, Sarah felt a mix of relief and apprehension wash over her. She'd been so certain, but now, face-to-face with their suspect, a nagging feeling of uncertainty crept in.

"You've got it all wrong," Thompson said, his voice trembling. "I didn't kill anyone. I was trying to protect her."

Sarah's brow furrowed. "Protect who?"

Just then, her radio crackled to life. "Detective Mitchell, we've got something. You need to see this immediately."

Sarah's eyes widened, her gaze locked on Thompson. What had they missed?

Chapter 15

The interrogation room door flew open with a bang, startling John from his hunched position at the metal table. Sarah Mitchell strode in, her eyes blazing with determination. The fluorescent lights cast harsh shadows across her face as she slammed a file onto the table.

"Enough games, John. Tell me what happened to Evelyn Langdon," Sarah demanded, her voice sharp as a knife's edge.

John leaned back in his chair, arms crossed defensively. "I don't know what you're talking about, detective." His eyes darted to the mirrored wall, then back to Sarah's face.

Sarah's jaw clenched. This guy wasn't going to break easily, but she'd cracked tougher nuts before. She pulled out the chair across from John, the metal legs scraping loudly against the concrete floor.

"Cut the crap," she said, leaning forward. "We both know you were there the night Evelyn died. The question is why."

John's expression remained impassive, but Sarah caught the slight twitch of his eye. Got him, she thought.

"I've got nothing to say," John muttered, looking away.

Sarah suppressed a smile. His evasion told her more than any confession could. She just needed to keep pushing.

"Really? Because your fingerprints say otherwise," Sarah bluffed, tapping the file folder. "Why don't you tell me your side of the story before things get worse for you?"

John's gaze snapped back to her, a flicker of uncertainty crossing his face. "You're lying," he said, but his voice lacked conviction.

Sarah leaned back, crossing her arms to mirror John's posture. "Am I? You seem awfully nervous for an innocent man, John."

She watched him carefully, noting the beads of sweat forming on his brow, the way his fingers drummed nervously on his bicep. He was close to breaking, she could feel it.

"Look," Sarah said, softening her tone slightly, "I'm not here to railroad you. I just want the truth. Help me understand what happened that night."

John's eyes met hers, searching for any sign of deception. Sarah held his gaze steadily, letting him see her sincerity. For a long moment, the room was silent save for the soft hum of the air conditioning.

Finally, John's shoulders slumped. "Alright," he said quietly. "I'll tell you what I know. But you have no idea what you're getting into, detective."

Sarah leaned forward, her heart racing with anticipation. She was about to blow this case wide open, she could feel it. "Try me," she said, her voice barely above a whisper.

Sarah reached into the manila folder she'd brought with her, pulling out a glossy photograph. She slid it across the table towards John, her eyes never leaving his face.

"Recognize this?" she asked, tapping the image with her index finger.

John's eyes widened almost imperceptibly as he looked down at the photo. It showed a bloody handprint on a polished wooden surface - unmistakably the one from Evelyn Langdon's study.

"This handprint," Sarah continued, her voice steady and matter-of-fact, "matches yours, John. We found it at the crime scene."

She watched as John's adam's apple bobbed, his jaw clenching. He's trying to stay calm, she thought, but I can see right through him.

"That's some pretty damning evidence," Sarah said, leaning back in her chair. "And it's just the tip of the iceberg. We've got more, John. A lot more."

John's eyes darted around the room, as if searching for an escape. Sarah could almost see the wheels turning in his head, weighing his options.

"Look," she said, her tone softening slightly. "I know you're in deep here. But right now, you've got a chance to come clean. To tell your side of the story. That chance won't last forever."

For a long moment, John was silent. Sarah held her breath, waiting. Then, finally, he spoke.

"Alright," he said, his voice barely above a whisper. "I did it. I killed Evelyn Langdon."

Sarah felt a surge of triumph, but kept her face neutral. "Why?" she asked simply.

John shook his head, a bitter laugh escaping his lips. "Does it matter? I did it, that's what you wanted to hear, right?"

"Who hired you, John?" Sarah pressed, leaning forward.

Fear flashed in John's eyes. "I can't tell you that," he said quickly. "They'd kill me if I talked."

Sarah's mind raced. Who could inspire such fear in a hardened criminal like John Blackwood?

"We can protect you," she offered, but John was already shaking his head.

"You have no idea what you're dealing with," he said, his voice low and urgent. "Trust me, detective. Some stones are better left unturned."

Sarah's eyes narrowed, her analytical mind kicking into high gear. She studied John's face, noting the beads of sweat on his forehead and the slight tremor in his hands. Fear was radiating off him in waves.

"John," she said, her voice firm but not unkind, "I understand you're scared. But right now, I'm your best shot at staying alive. Whoever hired you, they're going to realize you've been caught. How long before they decide you're a liability?"

John's eyes widened slightly, and Sarah knew she'd struck a nerve. She pressed on, "Give me something. Anything that could point us in the right direction."

John hesitated, his gaze darting to the two-way mirror behind Sarah. She could almost see the internal struggle playing out on his face.

"I... I can't give you a name," he finally said, his voice barely above a whisper. "But there was something. A cufflink. The guy who hired me, he always wore these fancy cufflinks. Gold, with some kind of bird design."

Sarah's heart raced. It wasn't much, but it was a lead. "Can you describe the bird?" she asked, trying to keep the excitement out of her voice.

As John began to describe the intricate design, Sarah's mind wandered to her team. She pictured them hunched over computers, sifting through mountains of data. Phone records, financial transactions, anything that could link Robert Langdon to this heinous crime.

A small part of her wished she was there with them, piecing together the puzzle. But she knew her place was here, in this room, carefully extracting every scrap of information she could from John Blackwood.

"One last thing, John," Sarah said, refocusing on the man in front of her. "Did you ever meet with your employer in person? Any details about the location could be crucial."

Sarah's phone buzzed insistently in her pocket, interrupting John's hesitant response. With an apologetic nod, she stepped out of the interrogation room, her heart pounding with anticipation.

"Talk to me," she answered, her voice low and urgent.

"Sarah, you need to see this," her colleague, Mark, said breathlessly. "We've uncovered a series of transactions between Robert Langdon and John Blackwood. It's... it's damning."

Sarah's eyes widened, her free hand clenching into a fist. "I'm on my way," she said, ending the call.

Moments later, she burst into the evidence room, where her team huddled around a computer screen. The air was thick with tension and the faint scent of stale coffee.

"Show me," Sarah demanded, leaning over Mark's shoulder.

He pointed to a series of highlighted entries on the screen. "Look here. Five separate wire transfers from an offshore account linked to Robert, directly to John. The last one was just three days before Evelyn's murder."

Sarah's mind raced, connecting the dots. "This is it," she breathed. "The link we've been looking for."

She straightened up, addressing her team. "Okay, people, listen up. We've got our smoking gun, but we need more. Robert's smart, and he's got resources. We need to build an airtight case."

Detective Rodriguez chimed in, his voice gruff with fatigue. "What about witnesses? Anyone who might have seen them together?"

Sarah nodded, her brow furrowed in concentration. "Good thinking. We'll need to re-interview the staff at Evelyn's estate. Someone must have noticed something suspicious."

As her team buzzed with renewed energy, Sarah's mind drifted to Robert Langdon. She could almost picture him, impeccably dressed as always, his charming smile hiding a web of deceit. How long had he been planning this? How deep did his resentment towards his mother run?

"What about motive?" she mused aloud. "We know Robert and Evelyn had a strained relationship, but murder? That's a big leap."

Mark looked up from his computer. "Maybe it wasn't just about their relationship. Evelyn was worth millions. With her gone, Robert stands to inherit everything."

Sarah nodded slowly, the pieces falling into place. "Greed and resentment. A deadly combination."

She took a deep breath, steeling herself for the challenge ahead. "Alright, team. We've got our work cut out for us. Let's build this case, piece by piece. Robert Langdon may think he's untouchable, but we're about to prove him wrong."

Sarah stood up, her eyes scanning the determined faces of her team. "Alright, let's divide and conquer," she said, her voice radiating authority. "Mark, I need you to dig deeper into those financial records. Follow every transaction, no matter how small. Rodriguez, you're on witness duty. Start with the estate staff, but cast a wider net. Check local businesses, delivery services, anyone who might have seen Robert and John together."

She turned to her youngest detective. "Thompson, you're our tech expert. I want you combing through their digital footprints. Emails, text messages, social media - anything that might connect them."

As Sarah doled out assignments, her mind raced with possibilities. Robert's charming facade flashed before her eyes, and she couldn't help but wonder how many people he'd fooled over the years.

"What about me?" Detective Lisa Chen asked, her pen poised over her notepad.

Sarah met her gaze. "You and I are going to pay a visit to Robert's inner circle. Friends, colleagues, maybe even his therapist if we can get access. Someone must have noticed a change in his behavior."

As the team dispersed, Sarah felt a familiar knot of tension in her stomach. She knew the road ahead would be fraught with obstacles.

Her suspicions proved correct when Rodriguez burst into her office an hour later, frustration etched on his face. "We've hit a wall with the witnesses," he reported, running a hand through his hair. "The estate staff are clamming up. They're scared, Sarah."

Sarah leaned back in her chair, her mind working overtime. "Scared of what? Or whom?"

Rodriguez shook his head. "They won't say. But I got the feeling they've been threatened. One of the maids was on the verge of talking, then suddenly went pale and refused to say another word."

Sarah felt a chill run down her spine. This was bigger than they'd initially thought. "Looks like our unknown mastermind is casting a long shadow," she murmured, more to herself than to Rodriguez.

She stood up, determination hardening her features. "We need to reassure these witnesses. Offer protection if necessary. Whatever it takes to get them to talk."

As Rodriguez nodded and left, Sarah turned to stare out the window. The city sprawled before her, hiding countless secrets. Somewhere out there, Robert Langdon was going about his day, perhaps believing he'd gotten away with murder.

"Not for long," Sarah whispered, her reflection steely-eyed in the glass. "We're coming for you, Robert. No matter what it takes."

Sarah's eyes narrowed as she scanned the stack of financial records on her desk. Something didn't add up. She reached for her phone, dialing quickly.

"Rodriguez, I need you to cross-reference these transactions with Robert's known aliases," she said, her voice taut with anticipation.

As she hung up, a knock at her door drew her attention. Detective Chen entered, looking tired but determined.

"Any luck with the bartender?" Sarah asked, studying Chen's face.

Chen sighed, shaking her head. "He's still refusing to talk. But I noticed something interesting. Every time I mentioned the night of the murder, his eyes would dart to the corner of the bar."

Sarah leaned forward, her interest piqued. "The corner? Was there anything significant there?"

"Just an old jukebox," Chen replied. "But I got the feeling it meant something to him."

Sarah stood up, her mind racing. "Good catch, Chen. Let's go back there. I want to take a closer look at that jukebox."

As they left the precinct, Sarah couldn't shake the feeling that they were on the verge of a breakthrough. She glanced at Chen, noting the determined set of her colleague's jaw.

"What are you thinking, Sarah?" Chen asked as they drove.

Sarah's lips curved into a small smile. "I'm thinking Robert Langdon isn't as clever as he believes. Everyone slips up eventually, and I have a hunch we're about to find his mistake."

The tension in the car was palpable as they neared their destination, both detectives acutely aware that they were inching closer to unraveling the web of lies surrounding Evelyn's murder.

Sarah's fingers drummed against the steering wheel as they pulled up to the bar. The neon sign flickered weakly in the early evening light, casting an eerie glow across the empty parking lot.

"Ready?" she asked Chen, her eyes scanning the area for any signs of trouble.

Chen nodded, her hand instinctively checking her holster. "Always."

They entered the dimly lit establishment, the smell of stale beer and cigarettes assaulting their senses. Sarah's gaze immediately locked onto the old jukebox in the corner.

"There it is," she murmured, striding towards it with purpose.

As they approached, Sarah's keen eyes swept over every inch of the machine. Something about its placement seemed off.

"Chen, does this look... crooked to you?" she asked, running her hand along the side of the jukebox.

Chen squinted, then nodded. "Yeah, it does. Like it's been moved recently."

Sarah's heart rate quickened. "Help me pull it out."

With a grunt of effort, they managed to slide the heavy machine away from the wall. Sarah's breath caught in her throat as she spotted something wedged behind it.

"Chen, look," she whispered, reaching down to retrieve a small, leather-bound notebook.

As Sarah flipped it open, her eyes widened. Inside were meticulous notes detailing payments, dates, and coded names. One entry, in particular, made her blood run cold:

"R.L. - Final installment - E.L. problem solved."

Sarah's mind raced, connecting the dots. R.L. Robert Langdon. E.L. Evelyn Langdon.

"We've got him," she breathed, a mix of triumph and dread washing over her.

Just then, the bar's door creaked open. Sarah whirled around, notebook clutched tightly in her hand, to find herself face to face with Robert Langdon himself.

His charming smile faltered as he took in the scene before him, his eyes darting from Sarah to the displaced jukebox to the damning evidence in her grasp.

"Detective Mitchell," he said, his voice strained. "What an... unexpected pleasure."

Chapter 16

The front door of Robert Langdon's mansion splintered as Sarah Mitchell's team burst through, guns drawn. Sarah's heart pounded as she led the charge into the opulent foyer, her keen eyes scanning for their target.

"Robert Langdon!" she shouted, her voice echoing off the marble floors. "NYPD! Show yourself!"

A crash from upstairs sent Sarah sprinting up the sweeping staircase, taking the steps two at a time. Her mind raced. This was it - the culmination of months of investigation. She couldn't let Robert slip away now.

She rounded the corner and skidded to a stop outside a set of heavy oak doors. With a nod to her team, Sarah kicked them open.

Robert stood frozen by the window, silhouetted against the fading evening light. His usual poise was gone, replaced by wide-eyed panic.

"It's over, Robert," Sarah said, leveling her gaze at him. Her voice was steady despite her racing pulse. "Step away from the window."

Robert's eyes darted around the room like a cornered animal. "Detective Mitchell," he said, forcing a smile that didn't reach his eyes. "To what do I owe this rather dramatic entrance?"

Sarah advanced slowly, never breaking eye contact. "I think you know exactly why we're here." She felt a grim satisfaction as uncertainty flickered across Robert's face. Got you, she thought.

"I'm afraid I don't," Robert replied, but his voice had lost its usual smooth confidence. "Perhaps you'd care to enlighten me?"

Sarah's lips curved in a humorless smile. "Oh, I intend to. But first - hands where I can see them, Robert. Now."

As Robert reluctantly raised his hands, Sarah allowed herself a moment of triumph. Months of sleepless nights and relentless pursuit had led to this moment. Justice for Evelyn was finally within reach.

But as she met Robert's gaze, Sarah felt an unexpected pang of empathy. Behind the polished facade, she glimpsed a flicker of the scared little boy who had never felt good enough. For just a heartbeat, Sarah's resolve wavered.

Then she steeled herself, pushing the feeling aside. Whatever Robert's reasons, he had to answer for what he'd done. With practiced efficiency, Sarah pulled out her handcuffs.

"Robert Langdon," she said, her voice ringing with finality, "you're under arrest for the murder of Evelyn Langdon."

Robert's composed facade cracked for a moment, his eyes widening in shock before he quickly regained control. "Murder? That's absurd," he scoffed, his voice taking on a defensive edge. "My mother died of natural causes. You have no grounds for this accusation."

Sarah raised an eyebrow, her piercing gaze never leaving Robert's face. "Is that so? Then perhaps you can explain this." She nodded to one of her team members, who produced a sealed evidence bag containing a crumpled piece of paper.

Robert's eyes darted to the bag, a flicker of recognition crossing his features before he masked it. "I don't know what that is," he said, his words coming out slightly too fast.

"No?" Sarah's tone was deceptively casual. "It's a draft of your mother's new will, found hidden in your study. A will that would have left you with nothing, Robert. Quite a motive, wouldn't you say?"

Robert's jaw clenched, his carefully manicured nails digging into his palms. "This is preposterous. I had no knowledge of any new will."

Sarah took a step closer, her voice low and intense. "We both know that's not true. Your fingerprints are all over it, Robert. And that's just the beginning of what we have."

For a moment, Robert seemed to deflate, the weight of his secrets visibly pressing down on him. But then he straightened, adjusting his tie with trembling hands. "I want my lawyer," he said, his voice barely above a whisper.

As Sarah began to read him his rights, she couldn't help but notice the conflict in Robert's eyes - a mix of fear, relief, and something that looked almost like regret. The case was far from over, but Sarah knew they had finally cracked the polished veneer of Robert Langdon.

Sarah's piercing gaze bore into Robert, her voice steady and resolute. "Your lawyer can't save you from the truth, Robert. We both know what really happened that night."

Robert's composure crumbled further, his once-immaculate suit now wrinkled and damp with sweat. He ran a shaky hand through his hair, eyes darting around the opulent living room as if searching for an escape.

"You don't understand," he muttered, his usual charm replaced by raw desperation. "She was going to take everything from me. Everything I've worked for..."

Sarah leaned in, her tone softening slightly but losing none of its intensity. "Tell me why, Robert. Help me understand."

Robert's breath hitched, his shoulders slumping. "She never thought I was good enough," he said, his voice barely audible. "No matter what I achieved, it was never enough for her."

Sarah nodded, encouraging him to continue. Robert's facade cracked entirely, words spilling out in a torrent.

"I couldn't bear the thought of losing it all," he confessed, eyes glistening. "The pressure, the expectations... I just wanted to be free."

As Robert's trembling voice filled the room with his reluctant admission, Sarah felt a mix of triumph and unexpected sympathy. She had dismantled his defenses, but the vulnerable man before her was a far cry from the polished suspect she'd pursued.

Sarah's piercing eyes softened slightly as she studied Robert's crumpled form. The luxurious living room suddenly felt stifling, the expensive artwork on the walls a stark contrast to the broken man before her.

"Tell me about your childhood, Robert," Sarah prompted gently, her voice losing its sharp edge. "What was it like growing up with your mother?"

Robert's gaze flickered to a framed photo on the mantle – a young boy with a forced smile standing next to a stern-looking woman. He swallowed hard.

"Perfect on the outside, suffocating on the inside," he said bitterly. "Every day was a test. Every achievement met with 'You can do better.' I was never allowed to just... be a kid."

Sarah nodded, her own memories of a demanding father flashing briefly through her mind. "That must have been difficult," she offered, her tone empathetic but still professional.

Robert looked up, surprise flickering across his face at her understanding. "I thought if I became successful enough, rich enough, she'd finally be proud. But nothing was ever enough for her."

As he spoke, Sarah noticed his hands fidgeting with his expensive watch – a nervous habit at odds with his usual polished demeanor. She recognized the weight of expectations he carried, even as her resolve to see justice done remained firm.

"I see now how that pressure shaped you, Robert," Sarah said quietly. "But it doesn't excuse what happened to your mother."

Robert's shoulders sagged further. "I know," he whispered, the fight finally draining out of him. "I just... I couldn't see any other way out."

Robert's composure finally crumbled, his carefully constructed facade shattering like glass. Tears welled in his expressive eyes, spilling down his chiseled cheeks as years of pent-up emotion burst forth.

"I never wanted to hurt her," he choked out, his usually articulate speech faltering. "But I felt so trapped, so... suffocated. Every decision, every moment of my life was orchestrated to meet her impossible standards."

Sarah watched silently, her body tense but her expression softening as Robert's raw vulnerability filled the opulent living room.

"The night it happened," Robert continued, his voice barely above a whisper, "she'd torn apart my latest business proposal. Said I was wasting my potential. And something just... snapped."

He ran a trembling hand through his perfectly coiffed hair, disheveling it. "In that moment, I saw a future stretching out before me – decades more of never being good enough, of always falling short. And I couldn't bear it."

Sarah leaned forward slightly, her voice gentle but probing. "So you saw murder as your only option?"

Robert laughed bitterly, the sound harsh and broken. "Option? No, it wasn't a calculated choice. It was... desperation. A primal need to break free, to finally breathe."

He looked down at his hands, as if seeing them for the first time. "I told myself it was justified. That I was reclaiming my life, my happiness. But now..." His voice trailed off, heavy with regret.

"Now?" Sarah prompted softly.

Robert met her gaze, his eyes haunted. "Now I realize I've become everything she feared I would be. A failure. A disappointment. A murderer."

Sarah inhaled sharply, the weight of Robert's confession settling over the room like a heavy fog. Her team members exchanged stunned glances, their expressions a kaleidoscope of emotions - shock, disbelief, and a flicker of sympathy for the broken man before them.

Detective Johnson, usually stoic, whispered, "Jesus Christ," under his breath, shaking his head in disbelief.

Sarah's mind raced, processing the gravity of the situation. She'd solved countless cases, but never had a confession hit her quite like this. Her voice, when she finally spoke, was steady but tinged with a complexity of emotions.

"Robert," she said, her piercing gaze fixed on him, "I appreciate your honesty. But you understand that regardless of your reasons, what you did was unforgivable."

Robert nodded numbly, his shoulders slumped in defeat. "I know," he whispered.

Sarah turned to her team, her expression hardening with renewed determination. "Let's wrap this up," she ordered, her voice carrying the weight of justice.

As her colleagues moved to secure the scene, Sarah approached Robert, handcuffs at the ready. "Robert Langdon, you're under arrest for the murder of Evelyn Langdon," she stated firmly.

The metallic click of the handcuffs echoed through the room, a stark contrast to the luxurious surroundings. As Sarah led him out, she couldn't help but reflect on the tragic irony of it all - a life of privilege ending in the back of a police car.

"You have the right to remain silent," Sarah began, reciting the Miranda rights with a mix of professionalism and an underlying current of empathy. As they stepped out into the cool night air, Sarah cast one last glance at the imposing mansion behind them, a silent witness to years of hidden turmoil and one fateful act of desperation.

Chapter 17

Dr. Elizabeth Shaw took a deep breath as she approached the witness stand, her heels clicking softly against the polished floor. The courtroom fell silent, all eyes fixed on her as she settled into the chair. She smoothed her charcoal gray blazer, a gesture that belied the flutter of nerves in her stomach.

"Please state your name and occupation for the record," the prosecutor requested.

"Dr. Elizabeth Shaw, criminal psychologist," she replied, her voice steady and clear.

As she glanced around the packed courtroom, Dr. Shaw could feel the weight of expectation hanging in the air. The jury leaned forward slightly, pens poised over notepads. In the gallery, she caught sight of Robert's mother, her face a mask of anguish. Poor woman, Dr. Shaw thought. She has no idea what's coming.

The judge, a stern-faced woman with salt-and-pepper hair, peered down at Dr. Shaw over her reading glasses. "You may proceed with your questioning, counselor," she intoned.

Dr. Shaw's gaze swept over to the defendant's table, where Robert sat hunched beside his lawyer. His eyes met hers for a brief moment before darting away. She felt a pang of sympathy, despite herself. So much pain in those eyes.

"Dr. Shaw," the prosecutor began, pacing before the witness stand. "In your expert opinion, what factors contributed to the defendant's decision to—"

A sudden cough from the jury box interrupted the question. Dr. Shaw watched as a middle-aged man fumbled for a water bottle, his face reddening as he tried to stifle the cough. She offered him a small, reassuring smile. It's alright, she wanted to tell him. We're all human here.

As the coughing subsided and attention returned to her, Dr. Shaw took another steadying breath. Here we go, she thought. Time to shine a light on the darkness.

Dr. Shaw leaned forward slightly, her voice clear and authoritative as she began to speak. "To understand Robert's actions, we must first understand his psychological landscape. For over three decades, I've specialized in criminal psychology, studying the intricate web of factors that lead individuals to commit heinous acts."

She paused, allowing her words to sink in. The courtroom hung on her every word, the air thick with anticipation.

"In Robert's case," she continued, "we're dealing with a perfect storm of deep-seated unhappiness and overwhelming pressure." Dr. Shaw's eyes flickered briefly to Robert, who seemed to shrink further into his chair.

The prosecutor nodded, encouraging her to elaborate. "Can you explain the source of this pressure, Dr. Shaw?"

"Certainly," she replied, her tone softening slightly. "From a young age, Robert was subjected to extraordinarily high expectations, primarily from his mother. These weren't just typical parental hopes for success, but a relentless demand for perfection in every aspect of his life."

As she spoke, Dr. Shaw couldn't help but notice Robert's mother in the gallery, her face a mix of disbelief and growing horror. Poor woman probably never realized the impact of her actions, she thought.

"This constant pressure," Dr. Shaw continued, "coupled with an inability to ever truly meet these impossible standards, created a deep well of resentment and self-doubt within Robert. He became a man perpetually at war with himself, outwardly successful but inwardly crumbling."

The prosecutor leaned against the witness stand. "And how did this internal conflict manifest in his decision to hire a hitman?"

Dr. Shaw took a moment to gather her thoughts. "In Robert's mind, eliminating his mother became a twisted form of self-preservation. He saw it as the only way to free himself from the crushing weight of her expectations."

As she spoke these words, a collective gasp rippled through the courtroom. Dr. Shaw's heart ached for the pain on display – Robert's, his mother's, and the palpable shock of those present. But she knew her duty was to the truth, no matter how difficult it might be to hear.

Dr. Shaw's gaze shifted to John Blackwood, sitting stone-faced beside Robert. Her voice softened as she continued, "Now, regarding John's willingness to participate in this crime, we must consider the complex interplay of his past experiences and psychological state."

She leaned forward slightly, her eyes scanning the courtroom. "John's troubled history, marked by a life lived on the fringes of society, created a perfect storm of vulnerability and desensitization to violence."

John's jaw clenched, his piercing eyes fixed on Dr. Shaw. She recognized the look – a mixture of defiance and barely concealed pain.

"His pattern of isolation and mistrust," Dr. Shaw explained, "likely stemmed from early experiences of betrayal or abandonment. This made him susceptible to manipulation, especially by someone offering a sense of purpose or belonging."

A murmur rippled through the courtroom. Dr. Shaw noticed Robert's family, their faces a canvas of conflicting emotions – shock, grief, and a dawning realization. John's side of the gallery remained eerily empty, save for a lone figure in the back, head bowed.

"It's important to understand," she continued, her tone gentle yet firm, "that John's participation doesn't excuse his actions. Rather, it provides context for the perfect storm of circumstances that led to this tragedy."

As she spoke, John's stoic facade cracked ever so slightly. For a brief moment, Dr. Shaw caught a glimpse of the vulnerable man beneath the hardened exterior.

The prosecutor, Sarah Daniels, rose from her seat, her crisp navy suit a stark contrast to the worn wooden benches. She approached the evidence table with measured steps, her heels clicking against the polished floor.

"Your Honor," she began, her voice clear and confident, "the prosecution would like to present Exhibit A."

She held up a sealed evidence bag containing a crumpled piece of paper. "This note, found in the defendant Robert Langdon's home office, outlines a detailed plan for the murder of his mother."

Robert's composed demeanor faltered for a moment, his fingers tightening on the edge of the defense table. The judge, a stern-faced woman in her sixties, leaned forward, her eyes narrowing as she examined the evidence.

"We also have phone records," Sarah continued, producing another document, "showing multiple calls between Mr. Langdon and Mr. Blackwood in the days leading up to the attempted murder."

John shifted in his seat, his intense gaze fixed on the prosecutor. His lips pressed into a thin line, the only visible sign of his discomfort.

The judge nodded, her voice crisp as she addressed the courtroom. "The evidence is admitted. Please proceed, Ms. Daniels."

As Sarah continued her presentation, Robert's mind raced. He thought, "How could I have been so careless? That note... I should have destroyed it." His heart pounded, each piece of evidence feeling like another nail in his coffin.

The tension in the courtroom was palpable, hanging heavy in the air like an impending storm. Robert glanced at John, their eyes meeting for a brief moment. In that instant, a flicker of understanding passed between them – they were in this together, for better or worse.

Dr. Elizabeth Shaw's words hung in the air, their weight palpable as the jurors leaned forward, captivated by her testimony. She adjusted her glasses, her eyes scanning the courtroom before continuing.

"Robert's resentment towards his mother wasn't born overnight," she explained, her tone both authoritative and compassionate. "It was a slow-burning fire, fueled by years of perceived inadequacy and the crushing weight of unfulfilled expectations."

Robert's jaw clenched, his gaze fixed on the polished surface of the defense table. Dr. Shaw's words seemed to peel back layers of his psyche, exposing raw nerves he'd long tried to ignore.

"And John," Dr. Shaw continued, her voice softening, "his willingness to participate stems from a complex interplay of financial desperation and a misguided sense of loyalty."

John's eyes darted to Dr. Shaw, a flicker of recognition crossing his face. She'd seen through him, laying bare the motivations he'd barely admitted to himself.

As Dr. Shaw concluded her testimony, a low murmur rippled through the courtroom. The prosecuting attorney, Sarah Daniels, allowed herself a small smile. "No further questions, Your Honor."

The defense attorney, Mark Thompson, rose quickly, his face set in determination. "Dr. Shaw," he began, his voice sharp, "isn't it possible that your analysis is colored by preconceived notions about my clients?"

Dr. Shaw met his gaze steadily. "I base my conclusions on years of experience and rigorous analysis, Mr. Thompson. My job is to understand, not to judge."

"And yet," Thompson pressed, pacing before the witness stand, "you've painted quite a damning picture of Mr. Langdon and Mr. Blackwood. How can we be sure your interpretation isn't simply confirming the prosecution's narrative?"

Dr. Shaw's lips quirked in a small smile. "Psychology isn't about confirming narratives, Mr. Thompson. It's about understanding the complex tapestry of human behavior. My testimony offers insight, not judgment."

As the cross-examination continued, Robert found his thoughts drifting. He marveled at how this stranger had so accurately dissected his innermost feelings. For a moment, he felt a strange sense of relief at being understood, quickly followed by a wave of dread at what that understanding might mean for his fate.

The tension in the courtroom was palpable as both the prosecution and defense prepared to deliver their closing arguments. Robert Langdon sat rigidly in his chair, his heart pounding. He glanced at John Blackwood beside him, noting the beads of sweat on his co-defendant's forehead.

Sarah Daniels, the prosecuting attorney, approached the jury box with measured steps. "Ladies and gentlemen," she began, her voice resonating through the hushed courtroom, "we've heard compelling evidence of a plot born from resentment and desperation. Mr. Langdon's unhappiness, his desire to please his mother at any cost, led him down a dark path."

Robert's jaw clenched. He thought, *Is that really all I am? A man desperate for mommy's approval?* The idea stung, but he couldn't entirely dismiss it.

"And Mr. Blackwood," Sarah continued, gesturing towards John, "a man with a troubled past, easily swayed by the promise of money. Together, they conspired to commit a heinous act."

Linda Carter, seated in the gallery, leaned forward, her brow furrowed with concern. She caught Robert's eye, offering a small, reassuring smile.

As the defense began their closing argument, Robert's mind wandered. He found himself thinking of his mother, Evelyn. *What would she think of me now?* he wondered, a mixture of anger and longing washing over him.

"My clients are not the cold-blooded conspirators the prosecution would have you believe," Mark Thompson argued passionately. "They are flawed men, yes, but not murderers."

As the arguments concluded, the judge turned to the jury. "You have heard the evidence. Now, it is time for you to deliberate and reach a verdict."

Robert's heart skipped a beat. This was it. The moment of truth approached, and he had never felt more uncertain about his future.

The courtroom fell into a tense silence as the jury filed out to begin their deliberations. Robert's eyes followed them, his heart pounding in his chest. He turned to his lawyer, Mark Thompson, who leaned in close.

"Stay calm," Mark whispered. "We've made a strong case."

Robert nodded, but his mind was racing. He glanced around the courtroom, taking in the faces of those present. Sarah Mitchell, the prosecutor, was shuffling papers at her desk, her expression unreadable. His sister Nancy sat in the gallery, her arms crossed, her gaze fixed on a spot on the wall.

"What do you think?" Robert murmured to Mark.

Mark sighed. "It's hard to say. Dr. Shaw's testimony was damaging, but we countered it well. Now we wait."

As the minutes ticked by, Robert found himself fidgeting in his seat. He thought of his mother, Evelyn, and wondered what she was doing at that moment. Was she following the trial? Did she care about the outcome?

The judge's voice cut through his thoughts. "We'll take a recess while the jury deliberates. Court is adjourned until they reach a verdict."

As people began to move, Robert caught sight of Linda Carter again. She gave him a small wave, and he felt a twinge of guilt. He turned away, unable to meet her eyes.

"Robert," Mark said, touching his arm. "Let's go over a few things while we wait."

Robert nodded, following his lawyer out of the courtroom. With each step, he felt the weight of his actions pressing down on him, wondering if this might be his last taste of freedom for a very long time.

As Robert followed Mark out of the courtroom, he couldn't help but chuckle softly to himself. "You know, Mark," he said, shaking his head, "when I was a kid, I always dreamed of being on TV. Never thought it'd be Court TV, though."

Mark raised an eyebrow, a hint of a smile playing at the corners of his mouth. "Well, at least you're dressed for the occasion. That tie really brings out the desperation in your eyes."

Robert snorted, grateful for the moment of levity. They made their way to a small conference room, the fluorescent lights buzzing overhead. As they sat down, Robert ran a hand through his hair, feeling the weight of the situation settling back onto his shoulders.

"So," he said, his voice tight, "what's our next move? I mean, besides praying for a miracle?"

Mark leaned forward, his expression serious but not unkind. "Look, Robert, I won't sugarcoat it. Dr. Shaw's testimony was tough. But we've got a few cards left to play."

Robert nodded, his mind drifting to thoughts of his mother. He wondered if she was watching, if she cared. A familiar mix of resentment and longing welled up inside him.

"You think my mother's following this circus?" he asked, trying to keep his tone light.

Mark's eyes softened. "I couldn't say. But Robert, right now, we need to focus on you. On getting through this."

Robert sighed, nodding. He glanced around the sterile room, thinking how different it was from the opulent offices he was used to. "You know," he said, a wry smile on his face, "I never thought I'd say this, but I actually miss my old cubicle right now."

Mark chuckled, then pulled out some papers. "Alright, let's go over our strategy for the closing arguments. We've got to make every word count."

As they dove into the details, Robert tried to push away thoughts of the jury, of his mother, of Linda's sad eyes. He focused on Mark's words, clinging to the hope that somehow, someway, this nightmare might still end in his favor.

Chapter 18

Sarah Mitchell stood outside Captain Reeves' office, her hand poised to knock. She took a deep breath, steeling herself for whatever was coming. Even after years on the force, being summoned still made her stomach flutter with nervous anticipation.

She rapped twice on the door, then entered at the gruff "Come in" from inside.

Captain Reeves looked up from his desk, his usually stern expression softening slightly as Sarah approached. "Detective Mitchell, have a seat."

Sarah perched on the edge of the chair, her back ramrod straight. "Is everything alright, sir?"

The captain leaned back, a hint of a smile playing at the corners of his mouth. "More than alright, Detective. I called you in here to commend you on your exceptional work on the Westbrook case."

Sarah blinked, caught off guard by the praise. She'd been expecting a reprimand, not recognition. "Thank you, sir. I was just doing my job."

"No, Mitchell. You went above and beyond. Your thoroughness and commitment to justice cracked a case that had us stumped for months." He pushed a folder across the desk. "This commendation will go in your file. You should be proud."

Sarah's cheeks warmed as she accepted the folder. "I appreciate that, Captain. But it was a team effort. I couldn't have done it without—"

"I know, I know," Reeves cut her off with a wave of his hand. "You're always quick to share credit. But this time, take the win. You earned it."

As Sarah left the office, folder clutched to her chest, she allowed herself a small smile. It felt good to be recognized, even if a part of her still bristled at the attention.

Across the bullpen, she spotted Kevin Johnson huddled with a group of officers. His confident stance and animated gestures caught her eye. This wasn't the same uncertain rookie she'd worked with months ago.

Sarah drifted closer, catching snippets of conversation.

"Alright, team," Kevin was saying, his voice steady and assured. "We've got a new case. Break-in at the art gallery on 5th. I want Johnston and Ramirez to canvas the area, see if any of the shops have security footage. Chen, you're with me at the scene."

The officers nodded, clearly responding to Kevin's leadership. As they dispersed, Sarah approached him.

"Nice work, Johnson," she said. "You seem to have things well in hand."

Kevin grinned, a touch of his old eagerness showing through. "Thanks, Detective Mitchell. I learned from the best." He paused, his expression growing more serious. "That last case... it taught me a lot. About police work, sure, but also about trusting my instincts and not being afraid to take charge when needed."

Sarah nodded, a surge of pride warming her chest. She'd had her doubts about Kevin initially, but he'd proven himself time and again. "Well, don't let me keep you. Sounds like you've got an art heist to solve."

As Kevin hurried off, Sarah watched him go, marveling at how much he'd grown. She glanced down at the commendation in her hands, then back at Kevin's retreating figure. Sometimes, she reflected, the real reward wasn't in the accolades, but in seeing the positive impact of your work on others.

Linda Carter sat across from a young woman, her warm brown eyes filled with compassion. The community center's small meeting room felt cozy, sunlight streaming through the windows and casting a soft glow on the worn furniture.

"Melissa, I know it's been difficult," Linda said gently, leaning forward. "But you've made so much progress. How are you feeling today?"

Melissa, her eyes red-rimmed and hands fidgeting in her lap, took a shaky breath. "I... I still have nightmares sometimes. About the break-in. But I'm trying those techniques you taught me."

Linda nodded encouragingly. "That's great, Melissa. Remember, healing takes time. You're doing wonderfully." She reached out, placing a reassuring hand on Melissa's arm. "Have you considered joining our support group? Many find it helpful to connect with others who've had similar experiences."

"I don't know," Melissa hesitated. "Talking about it in front of strangers..."

"It can be scary," Linda acknowledged, her voice warm. "But you'd be surprised how supportive everyone is. No pressure, though. We're here whenever you're ready."

As they continued talking, Linda's mind briefly flashed to the dozens of other victims affected by the recent string of burglaries. Each face, each story unique, yet all bound by a common thread of trauma. It was emotionally taxing work, but moments like these – seeing the flicker of hope in Melissa's eyes – made it all worthwhile.

Meanwhile, across town, Sarah Mitchell stood at her apartment window, lost in thought. The city sprawled before her, a maze of lights and shadows. She absently traced the outline of her detective badge, hanging from its usual spot by the door.

The weight of the recent case settled on her shoulders, heavier than she'd anticipated. Sarah closed her eyes, memories flooding back – the fear in the victims' eyes, the cold calculation of the perpetrator, the moment of triumph when justice was finally served.

"How does someone get to that point?" she murmured to herself, thinking of the burglar's twisted motivations. "All that anger, that resentment... festering for years."

She shook her head, feeling a mix of sadness and frustration. The case had forced her to confront the darkest aspects of human nature, but also reminded her of the resilience of the human spirit.

Opening her eyes, Sarah's gaze fell on a framed photo of her academy graduating class. Her younger self smiled back, full of idealism and determination. She'd seen so much since then, solved so many cases. Yet each one still affected her, still taught her something new about the complexities of human behavior.

"It's not just about catching the bad guys," Sarah reflected, her voice barely above a whisper. "It's about understanding why they do what they do. Maybe then we can prevent it from happening again."

She turned from the window, feeling both drained and oddly invigorated. Tomorrow would bring new challenges, new cases. But for now, Sarah allowed herself a moment of quiet reflection, acknowledging the toll of her chosen path while reaffirming her commitment to justice.

Sarah strode into the precinct's conference room, her eyes quickly scanning the familiar faces of her fellow detectives. The buzz of conversation quieted as she took her seat at the head of the table, her presence commanding attention without a word.

"Alright, team," she began, her voice clear and authoritative. "I want to share some insights from our recent case. It's crucial we understand not just what happened, but why."

Detective Rodriguez leaned forward, his brow furrowed. "You mean the burglar's motives?"

Sarah nodded, her piercing gaze meeting his. "Exactly. This wasn't just about greed or opportunity. It was years of resentment, of feeling wronged by society."

As she spoke, Sarah's mind flashed back to the interrogation room, the raw anger in the perpetrator's eyes. She suppressed a shudder, reminding herself to stay focused.

"Understanding these motivations isn't about sympathy," she continued, her tone firm. "It's about prevention. If we can identify these patterns early, we might stop the next crime before it happens."

Detective Chen raised her hand. "But how do we do that? We can't read minds."

Sarah allowed herself a small smile. "No, but we can learn to read behavior. Look for the signs, the patterns. It's not just about solving crimes; it's about understanding the human psyche."

As the discussion continued, Sarah felt a sense of pride in her team's engagement. They were asking thoughtful questions, sharing their own experiences. This, she thought, is how we grow stronger as investigators.

Meanwhile, across the precinct, Kevin Johnson stood nervously outside the office of Detective Sergeant Miller, a 30-year veteran of the force. Taking a deep breath, he knocked on the door.

"Come in," a gruff voice called out.

Kevin entered, his posture straight but his eyes betraying his nervousness. "Sergeant Miller, do you have a moment? I was hoping to get your advice on something."

Miller looked up from his paperwork, his weathered face softening slightly at Kevin's earnest expression. "Sure, kid. What's on your mind?"

Kevin sat down, leaning forward eagerly. "I've been thinking about the last case, sir. About how Detective Mitchell approached it. I want to learn to think like that, to see the bigger picture."

Miller nodded slowly, a hint of approval in his eyes. "Good instinct, Johnson. What specifically caught your attention?"

As Kevin began to explain, his initial nervousness faded, replaced by genuine enthusiasm. He peppered the sergeant with questions, soaking up every bit of wisdom the older man offered.

"Remember, Johnson," Miller said as their conversation wound down, "every case is a learning opportunity. Stay curious, stay hungry for knowledge. That's how you become a great detective."

Kevin stood up, feeling invigorated. "Thank you, sir. I really appreciate your time."

As he left the office, Kevin's mind was already racing with new ideas and perspectives. He couldn't wait for the next case, eager to apply what he'd learned and continue growing as an officer.

Linda Carter smoothed her auburn hair and surveyed the community center room with warm brown eyes. Folding chairs formed a circle, each one representing a life touched by the recent case. She took a deep breath, steadying herself for the emotional journey ahead.

As people began to trickle in, Linda greeted each with a gentle smile and a reassuring touch on the arm. "Welcome," she said softly to a young woman who hesitated at the doorway. "I'm Linda. We're glad you're here."

Once everyone was seated, Linda took her place in the circle. "Thank you all for coming," she began, her voice filled with warmth. "This is a safe space for us to share our experiences and support one another. Who would like to start?"

A middle-aged man cleared his throat. "I... I'm not sure how to move forward," he admitted, his voice cracking.

Linda nodded encouragingly. "That's a common feeling, Tom. Would you like to tell us more about what you're struggling with?"

As Tom spoke, Linda noticed others nodding in recognition. She thought to herself, 'This shared understanding is so powerful. It's the first step towards healing.'

The discussion flowed, punctuated by moments of tears and even tentative laughter. Linda guided the conversation with gentle prompts, her heart swelling with each small breakthrough.

Meanwhile, across town, Sarah Mitchell stood rigidly in her dress uniform, her sharp features set in a neutral expression as she faced a room full of her colleagues and superiors.

The police chief stepped forward, a commendation in his hands. "Detective Sarah Mitchell," he announced, "for your exceptional work and unwavering dedication in solving the Riverside case, we present you with this commendation."

As applause filled the room, Sarah accepted the award, her mind racing. 'This isn't just my victory,' she thought, her eyes scanning the faces of her team. 'We did this together.'

"Thank you, sir," Sarah said, her voice clear and steady. "I'm honored, but I couldn't have done this without the support and hard work of my entire team. This commendation belongs to all of us."

She paused, her piercing gaze sweeping the room. "Every member of this department contributed to solving this case. It's a testament to what we can achieve when we work together, when we refuse to give up, and when we remember why we do this job - to serve and protect our community."

As she stepped back, Sarah felt a mix of pride and humility. The weight of the commendation in her hands reminded her of the responsibility that came with it - to continue striving for justice, to keep pushing herself and her team to be better.

The ceremony concluded, but Sarah's mind was already on the next case, the next challenge. She knew that this recognition wasn't an endpoint, but a milestone in her ongoing journey as a detective.

Kevin Johnson stood at the edge of the crime scene, his keen eyes scanning the area. The flashing lights of police cruisers cast an eerie glow on the suburban street. He took a deep breath, feeling a newfound confidence coursing through him.

"Alright, let's approach this methodically," he said to his partner, Officer Martinez. "Remember what we learned from the Riverside case? Every detail matters."

Kevin ducked under the yellow tape, his mind racing with possibilities. He crouched near a discarded cigarette butt, carefully bagging it as evidence.

"Martinez, check the perimeter. Look for anything out of place, no matter how small," he instructed, his voice steady and assured.

As he stood, Kevin's gaze fell on a slightly ajar window. 'That's odd,' he thought. 'In this neighborhood, at this time of year?'

"Hey, Martinez," he called out. "Let's get forensics to dust that window frame. It might give us a lead."

Kevin felt a sense of pride wash over him. The lessons from his previous case were paying off, guiding his actions and sharpening his instincts.

Meanwhile, across town, Linda Carter sat in her office, surrounded by the warm glow of her desk lamp. A gentle knock on the door interrupted her thoughts.

"Come in," she called out, her voice warm and inviting.

The door opened, revealing Sarah, one of the women from her support group. Sarah's eyes were brimming with tears, but a smile played on her lips.

"Linda, I... I just wanted to thank you," Sarah began, her voice trembling. "Your guidance, your compassion... it's made such a difference in my life."

Linda stood up, moving around her desk to embrace Sarah. "Oh, sweetie, I'm so glad. You've done all the hard work yourself, you know."

Sarah shook her head, wiping away a tear. "No, Linda. You created a safe space for us. You helped us find our voices again. I don't know where I'd be without your support."

Linda felt a lump form in her throat. "That's what I'm here for," she said softly. "To help you all find your strength again."

As they talked, Linda's mind wandered to all the lives she'd touched, all the stories she'd heard. It reinforced her commitment to her work, reminding her why she chose this path in the first place.

Sarah Mitchell stood at the window of her apartment, gazing out at the twinkling city lights. Her reflection stared back at her, eyes intense and thoughtful. She absently fingered the badge on her belt, its weight a familiar comfort.

"It's not just about solving puzzles," she murmured to herself, her voice barely audible. "It's about the lives we touch, the justice we bring."

She turned away from the window, her gaze falling on a framed photo of a smiling family - the Johnsons, whose case she'd recently closed. Their gratitude had been overwhelming, almost uncomfortable for the usually stoic detective.

Sarah picked up the frame, a rare smile tugging at her lips. "This is why I do it," she thought. "To give voices to the voiceless, to right the wrongs."

Her phone buzzed, jolting her from her reverie. It was a text from Kevin.

"Hey Sarah, got a new recruit. Any advice?"

Sarah chuckled, typing back, "Remember how green you were? Pay it forward, rookie."

Across town, Kevin pocketed his phone, grinning at the recruit beside him. "Ready for your first case, Martinez?"

The young woman nodded eagerly, her eyes bright with anticipation. "Yes, sir!"

Kevin led her towards the crime scene, his stride confident. "Alright, let's start with the basics. What do you see?"

As Martinez began to list her observations, Kevin felt a surge of pride. He remembered being in her shoes, eager but unsure. Now, he was the one guiding, sharing his hard-earned wisdom.

"Good eye," he praised. "But remember, it's not just about what you see. It's about what you don't see. That's where the real story lies."

Linda Carter stood in the conference room, surrounded by her colleagues and superiors. The gentle hum of conversation filled the air, but Linda's attention was drawn to the large window overlooking the city. Sunlight streamed in, casting a warm glow over the room.

"Linda?" Her supervisor's voice pulled her from her thoughts. "Are you ready?"

Linda turned, smoothing her blouse nervously. "As ready as I'll ever be," she said with a soft chuckle.

The room fell silent as her supervisor addressed the group. "We're here today to recognize Linda Carter for her exceptional work in supporting those affected by the recent case."

Linda felt a flush creep up her neck as applause filled the room. She caught sight of her reflection in the window - her auburn hair neatly tucked behind her ears, her warm brown eyes wide with surprise.

"Linda's dedication and compassion have been instrumental in helping our community heal," her supervisor continued. "Her tireless efforts have not gone unnoticed."

As the applause died down, Linda stepped forward. "I... I'm truly honored," she began, her voice wavering slightly. "But this recognition belongs to all of us. We're a team, and together, we make a difference."

Across town, Sarah Mitchell sat at her desk, surrounded by stacks of files and sticky notes. Her piercing eyes scanned the documents before her, her brow furrowed in concentration.

"New case, new challenges," she muttered to herself, reaching for her coffee mug. She took a sip, grimacing at the cold liquid. How long had she been at this?

Sarah stood, stretching her stiff muscles. She moved to the whiteboard, picking up a marker. "Okay, Mitchell," she thought, "let's break this down."

As she began to sketch out a timeline, her phone buzzed. It was a text from Linda: "Just got an award at work. Wish you could've been here!"

Sarah smiled, typing back: "Congratulations, Linda. Well deserved."

She turned back to the whiteboard, her determination renewed. "Time to make a difference," she murmured, diving back into her work.

Five years later, the bustling precinct hummed with activity as Sarah strode through the bullpen, her steps purposeful and confident. She paused at Kevin's desk, a hint of a smile playing on her lips.

"Ready for the press conference, Detective Johnson?" she asked, her tone warm but professional.

Kevin looked up, his once boyish face now bearing the subtle lines of experience. "As ready as I'll ever be, Captain Mitchell," he replied with a grin. "Still can't believe we cracked this one."

Sarah nodded, her eyes gleaming with pride. "You led a solid investigation. It's your time to shine."

As they walked towards the conference room, Sarah's phone buzzed. She glanced at the screen, her expression softening. "It's Linda," she explained. "Says she's watching the live stream with her support group."

Kevin chuckled. "Some things never change, huh? She's still everyone's rock."

"That she is," Sarah agreed, her mind drifting to the case that had brought them all together years ago. "You know, sometimes I wonder how different things might have been if we hadn't solved that case."

They paused outside the conference room, the muffled sounds of reporters chattering filtering through the door.

"We did good work then," Kevin said, straightening his tie. "And we're still doing it now. Ready to face the wolves, Captain?"

Sarah squared her shoulders, her characteristic determination settling over her features. "Always," she replied, pushing open the door. As camera flashes erupted around them, she thought to herself, "We've come a long way, but there's still work to be done. And we'll do it, one case at a time."

Chapter 19

The key clicked in the lock, and Sarah Mitchell pushed open her front door with a weary sigh. The familiar scent of her apartment—a mix of lavender air freshener and old books—enveloped her as she stepped inside. She dropped her heavy work bag onto the couch with a soft thud, wincing at the dull ache in her shoulder.

"Home sweet home," she murmured, kicking off her sensible black shoes. They clattered against the baseboard, and Sarah felt a twinge of guilt for the mess. She'd tidy up later. Maybe.

Her stockinged feet padded across the hardwood floor as she made her way to the kitchen. The cool surface was a balm to her aching soles after a long day of pounding the pavement. Sarah reached for the coffee maker, her movements automatic after years of the same routine.

As she filled the carafe with water, Sarah's mind drifted back to the case she'd just closed. The faces of the victims, the perpetrator, the grieving families all swirled in her mind like a grim kaleidoscope.

"Focus, Mitchell," she chided herself, measuring out the coffee grounds. "It's over. You did your job."

The coffee maker gurgled to life, and soon the rich aroma of brewing coffee filled the air. Sarah inhaled deeply, feeling some of the tension in her shoulders release. She leaned against the counter, letting her eyes drift closed for a moment.

The case had been a tough one, even by her standards. A series of home invasions that had escalated to murder, leaving a community paralyzed with fear. Sarah had poured everything she had into solving it, working long hours and following every lead, no matter how small.

As the last drops of coffee fell into the pot, Sarah poured herself a mug, savoring the warmth that seeped through the ceramic and into her hands. She took a sip, the bitter flavor dancing across her tongue.

"Good work, detective," she told herself softly, a rare moment of self-praise. "You got the bastard."

But even as she said the words, Sarah knew the ghosts of this case would linger, joining the others that haunted her dreams. It was the price she paid for her dedication, for her relentless pursuit of justice. A price she'd gladly pay again and again if it meant bringing closure to those who needed it most.

Sarah's eyes fell on the stack of mail on the counter. With a sigh, she picked up the envelopes, idly flipping through them as she sipped her coffee.

"Bill, bill, junk... more junk," she muttered, tossing each onto the counter with a soft thwap. Her movements were mechanical, her mind still caught in the whirlwind of the investigation.

A cream-colored envelope caught her attention. Sarah paused, frowning at the unfamiliar handwriting. "What's this?" she murmured, setting down her mug to open it.

As she scanned the letter, her eyebrows shot up. "Well, I'll be damned," she said softly, a hint of a smile tugging at her lips. It was a thank you note from the victim's family.

Sarah's gaze lingered on the heartfelt words, her throat tightening. She set the letter down and picked up her coffee, padding into the living room. The worn leather armchair beckoned, and she sank into its familiar embrace with a weary sigh.

"You did good, Sarah," she told herself, echoing the letter's sentiment. "You made a difference."

But as she stared into the middle distance, the weight of the case settled over her like a heavy blanket. The faces of the victims, the fear in their eyes, the devastation of their families – it all came rushing back.

Sarah took another sip of coffee, her hands trembling slightly. "Get it together, Mitchell," she whispered, her voice barely audible in the quiet room. "It's over. You did your job."

Sarah closed her eyes, letting the faces of those involved in the investigation flood her mind. The grieving mother's tear-stained cheeks, the stoic father trying to hold it together for his family. Their pain was palpable, etched into her memory.

"Why?" she murmured, her brow furrowing. "What drives someone to inflict such suffering?"

The perpetrator's face swam into focus - eyes cold, devoid of remorse. Sarah shuddered, recalling their final interrogation.

"I had no choice," his words echoed in her mind. "They deserved it."

Sarah's eyes snapped open, her jaw clenching. "No one deserves that," she said firmly to the empty room.

She leaned back, contemplating the twisted path that led to such heinous acts. The abuse, the neglect, the years of bottled-up resentment that had finally exploded in violence.

A familiar ache bloomed in her chest as her thoughts turned inward. "You're not so different, are you?" she whispered to herself. The betrayal that had shaped her, the walls she'd built to protect herself - Sarah recognized the seeds of resentment all too well.

She took a deep breath, exhaling slowly. "But you chose differently," she reminded herself. "You chose justice, not vengeance."

Sarah's gaze fell on a framed photo of her mother, her expression softening. "You taught me that, didn't you, Mom? To heal, to forgive... even when it's hard."

She raised her mug in a silent toast. "Here's to breaking the cycle," Sarah said softly, a bittersweet smile playing on her lips. "One case at a time."

Sarah reached for the notepad and pen on her side table, her movements deliberate and purposeful. The weight of the pen in her hand felt reassuring, grounding her swirling thoughts.

"Alright," she murmured, tapping the pen against her chin. "Let's break this down."

She began to write, her neat handwriting filling the page with observations and insights.

"The trigger," Sarah muttered, underlining the word. "It always comes back to the trigger."

As she jotted down her thoughts, Sarah found herself speaking aloud, her voice barely above a whisper.

"Childhood trauma, unresolved grief, societal pressures..." She paused, her pen hovering over the paper. "But why does one person break while another bends?"

Sarah's brow furrowed as she continued writing, occasionally pausing to tap her pen against her lips. The act of putting her thoughts on paper seemed to clear the fog in her mind, bringing clarity to the complex web of motivations and circumstances she'd uncovered during the investigation.

After filling several pages, Sarah set the notepad aside and stood, stretching her arms above her head. Her gaze drifted to the bookshelf across the room, and she walked over, running her fingers along the spines of the books.

"Time to dig deeper," she said, pulling out a few volumes on psychology and criminal behavior.

Sarah settled back into her chair, balancing a hefty tome on her lap. As she flipped through the pages, her eyes scanned the text, occasionally pausing on a relevant passage.

"Interesting," she murmured, leaning in closer to read a paragraph on the psychology of revenge. "I wonder if our perpetrator fits this profile..."

She reached for her notepad again, scribbling down new observations and questions. The soft rustle of pages and the scratch of pen on paper filled the room as Sarah continued her personal investigation, determined to understand the depths of human nature that her work constantly revealed.

Sarah glanced up from her book, her eyes landing on a framed photograph on the nearby side table. The image of her late mother, smiling warmly, seemed to gaze back at her with a mixture of pride and concern. Sarah's expression softened, a wistful smile tugging at the corners of her mouth.

"Oh, Mom," she whispered, reaching out to touch the frame. "I wish you could see me now."

Her throat tightened as she remembered her mother's unwavering support of her career choice. "You always said I had a knack for solving puzzles," Sarah mused, her voice barely audible. "I guess you were right."

A bittersweet chuckle escaped her lips as she recalled her mother's words of wisdom. "Justice isn't just about catching the bad guys, Sarah," she mimicked her mother's gentle tone. "It's about understanding why people do what they do."

Sarah's fingers traced the outline of her mother's face in the photograph. "I'm trying, Mom. I really am."

She closed her eyes, inhaling deeply and exhaling slowly. The tension in her shoulders began to melt away as she focused on her breathing. In her mind's eye, she could almost feel her mother's comforting presence.

"One case at a time," Sarah murmured, her voice growing stronger. "That's how we make a difference."

As she opened her eyes, Sarah's gaze held a renewed sense of determination. She straightened her posture, squaring her shoulders as if preparing for battle.

"Alright," she said to herself, a hint of her usual tenacity creeping back into her voice. "Let's get back to work."

Sarah's gaze swept across her living room, taking in the scattered case files and discarded coffee mugs. With a determined nod, she began to tidy up, her actions purposeful and methodical.

"Time to put this one to bed," she muttered, gathering papers into neat stacks.

As she organized, Sarah's mind drifted to the case's complexities. She paused, holding a photo of the crime scene.

"What a mess," she sighed, tucking it away. "But it's over now."

Sarah moved to the kitchen, rinsing mugs and loading the dishwasher. The familiar routine brought a sense of normalcy.

"Clean space, clear mind," she recited her mother's old mantra, a small smile tugging at her lips.

Returning to the living room, Sarah straightened cushions and folded throw blankets. Each action felt like shedding the weight of the investigation.

"There," she said, surveying her now-tidy space. "That's better."

Sarah grabbed her keys, hesitating at the front door. She took a deep breath, hand on the doorknob.

"Ready or not, world," she murmured, opening the door.

Stepping onto her porch, Sarah's keen eyes scanned her quiet neighborhood. The setting sun cast a warm glow, and a gentle breeze carried the scent of blooming flowers.

"It's beautiful out here," she whispered, her voice tinged with wonder.

As she stood there, Sarah felt a newfound sense of purpose wash over her. The world seemed brighter, full of possibilities.

"There's still good out there," she reminded herself. "And I'm going to find it."

With a confident nod, Sarah stepped forward, ready to face whatever challenges lay ahead.

Chapter 20

Epilogue

One year had passed since the trial that shook the Langdon family to its core. Robert Langdon stood at the window of his high-rise apartment, gazing out at the city skyline as the setting sun painted the sky in hues of orange and pink. He took a sip of his whiskey, savoring the burn as it slid down his throat.

"It's been quite a year, hasn't it?" Nancy's voice broke through his reverie.

Robert turned to face his sister, who was perched on the edge of his leather sofa. Her dark hair was pulled back in its usual practical style, but there was a softness in her eyes that he hadn't seen in years.

"That's an understatement," he replied with a wry smile. "Sometimes I still can't believe it all happened."

Nancy nodded, her fingers tracing the rim of her wine glass. "The trial, the media circus, Mom's..." she trailed off, unable to finish the sentence.

Robert's chest tightened at the mention of their mother. Evelyn Langdon's breakdown in the courtroom had been splashed across every newspaper and gossip magazine for weeks. He could still hear her anguished cries echoing in his ears.

"Have you spoken to her recently?" he asked, trying to keep his voice neutral.

Nancy shook her head. "Not since she checked into the rehabilitation center. The doctors say she's making progress, but..." She shrugged, leaving the rest unsaid.

Robert moved to sit beside his sister, the leather creaking beneath his weight. He noticed the way Nancy's shoulders tensed slightly at his proximity, a reminder of the distance that had grown between them over the years.

"I keep thinking about what could have been different," he confessed, staring into the amber liquid in his glass. "If I had just stood up to her sooner, if I hadn't let her expectations consume me..."

Nancy reached out, hesitantly placing her hand on his arm. "We can't change the past, Rob. But maybe... maybe this is our chance to build something new."

Robert looked up, meeting his sister's gaze. For a moment, he saw a flicker of the closeness they had shared as children, before ambition and family pressure had driven them apart.

"I'd like that," he said softly, covering her hand with his own. "God knows, we could both use a fresh start."

As they sat there, the city lights twinkling to life outside the window, Robert felt a glimmer of hope stirring in his chest. The road ahead would be long and challenging, but for the first time in years, he felt ready to face it – not alone, but with his sister by his side.

The stark fluorescent lights buzzed overhead as Robert Langdon made his way down the sterile corridor of Oakdale Federal Correctional Institution. The clanging of metal doors and muffled voices echoed through the air, a constant reminder of his new reality.

"Langdon, you've got a visitor," a guard called out, gesturing towards the visitation room.

Robert's heart skipped a beat. "Who is it?" he asked, his usually smooth voice tinged with apprehension.

The guard shrugged. "Didn't say. Just get moving."

As Robert entered the room, he spotted John Blackwood seated at one of the metal tables, his scruffy appearance at odds with the pristine surroundings.

"John," Robert nodded, taking a seat across from him. "Didn't expect to see you here."

John's intense gaze met Robert's. "Figured we should talk, given our... shared circumstances."

Robert leaned back, his tailored prison uniform a far cry from his usual impeccable suits. "And what exactly is there to say?"

"Maybe nothing," John replied, his voice low and measured. "Or maybe everything."

Meanwhile, across town, Detective Sarah Mitchell stood in front of a cluttered evidence board, her piercing eyes scanning every detail. Photos of a young woman, crime scene snapshots, and scrawled notes covered the surface.

"What are we missing, Jenkins?" she asked her partner, not taking her eyes off the board.

Detective Jenkins sighed. "I don't know, Sarah. We've been over this a hundred times."

Sarah shook her head, her jaw set with determination. "There's something here. I can feel it." She pointed to a photo of the victim. "Melissa deserves justice, and I'm not going to stop until we find it."

Robert's eyes darted around the visitation room, taking in the stark white walls and the ever-present guard in the corner. He fidgeted with the cuff of his uniform, a habit born from months of confinement.

"I never thought I'd end up here," Robert admitted, his usual charm replaced by a somber introspection. "All those expectations, all that pressure... and look where it got me."

John leaned forward, his elbows resting on the table. "We all make choices, Langdon. Some just have bigger consequences than others."

Robert ran a hand through his hair, a ghost of his former polished appearance. "I've been attending these group therapy sessions," he said, his voice barely above a whisper. "It's... helping, I think. Makes me see things differently."

"Yeah?" John raised an eyebrow, a flicker of interest in his eyes. "How so?"

"I'm starting to understand why I did what I did," Robert replied, his gaze fixed on his hands. "All that resentment, that need to prove myself... it was eating me alive."

John nodded slowly, his usual guardedness softening. "I get that. Been doing some thinking myself. Turns out, there's a lot of time for that in here."

Robert looked up, surprised by the hint of vulnerability in John's tone. "And what have you been thinking about?"

John's eyes met Robert's, a mix of regret and determination visible. "About the people we hurt. About how I can make things right, even from in here."

Robert leaned back, a small smile tugging at his lips. "Sounds like we've both been on quite a journey."

"Journey's not over yet," John replied, his voice carrying a newfound sense of purpose. "But at least now, I think we're heading in the right direction."

Sarah Mitchell stood at her desk, her sharp eyes scanning the evidence board before her. The faces of victims and suspects stared back, a silent testament to her latest case. She reached for her coffee mug, only to find it empty.

"Burning the midnight oil again, Mitchell?" Detective Williams called from across the room.

Sarah's lips tightened into a thin smile. "You know me, always one more lead to chase."

As she turned back to her work, Sarah felt a familiar tightness in her chest. The case was taking its toll, each victim's story weighing on her more than she cared to admit.

Later that evening, Sarah found herself in Dr. Patel's office, her fingers absently tracing the pattern on the armchair.

"How are you sleeping, Sarah?" Dr. Patel asked, her voice gentle.

Sarah exhaled slowly. "Not great. The nightmares are back."

"Have you been trying those relaxation techniques we discussed?"

"I've... been painting again," Sarah admitted, a hint of embarrassment coloring her cheeks. "It helps, sometimes."

Dr. Patel nodded encouragingly. "That's excellent, Sarah. Creative outlets can be very therapeutic."

Sarah's mind drifted to her latest canvas, a swirl of dark blues and greys with a single streak of golden light. "I guess it's my way of making sense of things," she mused.

As she left the session, Sarah found herself reflecting on the past year. The case that had brought down Robert and John had changed her, sharpening her instincts but also opening old wounds.

"You can't save everyone," she whispered to herself, echoing Dr. Patel's words. "But you can make a difference, one case at a time."

With renewed determination, Sarah headed back to the precinct, ready to face whatever challenges lay ahead.

Sarah strode into the precinct, the familiar bustle and chatter washing over her. As she made her way to her desk, a young woman approached, eyes rimmed with red.

"Detective Mitchell?" The woman's voice quivered. "I'm Emily, Jason's sister."

Sarah's breath caught. Jason had been one of the victims in her last case. She gestured to a quiet corner. "Of course, Emily. How can I help you?"

Emily twisted her hands together. "I just... I wanted to thank you. For everything you did. For not giving up on Jason."

Sarah felt a lump form in her throat. "I'm just sorry we couldn't bring him home to you."

"But you brought us closure," Emily said, reaching out to squeeze Sarah's hand. "That means more than you know."

As Emily walked away, Sarah's partner, Mike, appeared at her elbow. "You okay?" he asked, concern etched on his face.

Sarah nodded, blinking rapidly. "Yeah, I'm good. Just... it hits home sometimes, you know?"

Mike's expression softened. "That's what makes you damn good at your job, Mitchell. You care."

Sarah managed a small smile, but as she turned back to her desk, she couldn't shake the weight of responsibility. Each case solved brought relief, but also a stark reminder of the lives forever changed.

She glanced at the framed photo on her desk – her and her sister, laughing at some long-forgotten joke. The glass was slightly smudged, a physical representation of the distance that had grown between them since Sarah had thrown herself into her work.

Sighing, Sarah pulled out her phone and typed out a quick message: "Hey sis, dinner this weekend? My treat."

As she hit send, Sarah realized that while she couldn't change the past, she could still shape her future. One case, one relationship at a time.

Robert Langdon stood in the community center's bustling kitchen, sleeves rolled up and hands submerged in soapy water. The clatter of dishes and hum of conversation filled the air as he scrubbed a particularly stubborn pot.

"Hey, Langdon!" called out Marcus, a fellow volunteer. "You missed a spot."

Robert chuckled, his eyes crinkling at the corners. "Thanks for the keen observation, Marcus. I'll make sure it sparkles just for you."

As he attacked the pot with renewed vigor, Robert's mind wandered. Just a year ago, he never would have imagined himself here, finding solace in such a mundane task. But now, each plate cleaned felt like a small step towards redemption.

Across the room, John Blackwood was carefully ladling soup into bowls, his intense gaze softened by the steam rising from the pot. A young woman approached, her eyes downcast.

"Excuse me," she mumbled, "is there any left?"

John's voice was gentle as he replied, "Of course. There's always enough here." He filled a bowl to the brim and handed it to her with a nod.

As the woman walked away, John caught Robert's eye. They shared a moment of understanding – both men acutely aware of the long road ahead, yet grateful for this opportunity to make a difference, however small.

Later, as they were hanging up their aprons, Robert turned to John. "You know, I never thought I'd say this, but I actually look forward to these shifts."

John's lips quirked in a half-smile. "Yeah, who'd have thought we'd find purpose in soup and suds?"

Robert laughed, a genuine sound that surprised even him. "Life's funny that way, I suppose. Speaking of which, are you going to that group session tomorrow?"

John hesitated, then nodded. "Yeah, I think I will. Talking about... everything. It helps, you know?"

"I do," Robert said softly. As they stepped out into the cool evening air, he added, "We can't change what we did, but maybe we can still do some good in this world."

John's eyes, usually so guarded, held a glimmer of hope. "One day at a time, right?"

"One day at a time," Robert agreed, looking up at the stars peeking through the city's haze. For the first time in a long while, the future didn't seem quite so bleak.

Robert and John walked side by side towards the prison block, their footsteps echoing in the quiet evening. The setting sun cast long shadows across the yard, painting the concrete in warm hues of orange and gold.

"You know," Robert mused, breaking the companionable silence, "I've been thinking about reaching out to Nancy."

John raised an eyebrow. "Your sister? I thought you two weren't on speaking terms."

Robert sighed, running a hand through his graying hair. "We weren't. Aren't. But after everything that's happened... I don't know. Maybe it's time to try and mend some fences."

They paused at the entrance to their cell block, the heavy metal door a stark reminder of their reality. John placed a hand on Robert's shoulder, his touch hesitant but sincere.

"For what it's worth, I think that's a good idea," he said. "Family's important. Even when it's complicated."

Robert nodded, a small smile tugging at his lips. "Thanks, John. I appreciate that."

As they entered the building, the familiar sounds and smells of prison life enveloped them. But somehow, it felt different now. There was a sense of purpose, of forward momentum, that hadn't been there before.

"You know," Robert said as they approached their cells, "I never thought I'd say this, but I'm actually looking forward to tomorrow's group session."

John chuckled softly. "Who are you and what have you done with Robert Langdon?"

Robert laughed, the sound echoing off the concrete walls. "I guess we're both changing, huh?"

As they parted ways for the night, Robert felt a warmth in his chest that had nothing to do with the evening's fading heat. It was hope, he realized. Small and fragile, but unmistakably there.

Lying on his bunk, Robert closed his eyes, picturing Nancy's face. Tomorrow, he decided. Tomorrow he'd write that letter. One step at a time towards a future he was finally beginning to believe in.

Sarah Mitchell sat at her desk, the soft glow of her computer screen illuminating her face in the dimly lit office. She leaned back in her chair, rubbing her tired eyes as she reflected on the case she had just closed. The weight of the past year's events settled heavily on her shoulders.

"Another one in the books," she murmured to herself, her voice barely audible in the quiet room.

Her partner, Detective Rodriguez, approached with two steaming cups of coffee. "Thought you could use this," he said, placing one on her desk.

Sarah smiled gratefully. "Thanks, Mike. Just wrapping up the paperwork."

As she reached for the cup, her eyes fell on a framed photo on her desk – a snapshot of her and her late sister, taken years ago. A pang of sadness mixed with a newfound understanding washed over her.

"You know," Sarah began, her gaze still fixed on the photo, "working on Robert and John's case... it's changed me."

Mike leaned against her desk, his eyebrows raised in curiosity. "How so?"

Sarah took a sip of coffee, gathering her thoughts. "I used to see things in black and white. Criminals were just... criminals. But now..."

She trailed off, her mind drifting to the complexities she'd uncovered during the investigation. The tangled web of emotions, the weight of unresolved resentment, the ripple effects of one person's actions on countless lives.

"Now?" Mike prompted gently.

Sarah met his eyes, a wry smile playing on her lips. "Now I see shades of gray everywhere. It's like... peeling back layers of an onion. There's always more beneath the surface."

She stood up, stretching her arms above her head. "Come on, I need some fresh air."

As they walked outside, the cool night breeze ruffled Sarah's hair. She took a deep breath, feeling some of the tension leave her body.

"You know what really got to me?" she said, her voice soft but clear in the quiet night. "Seeing how their unresolved issues from the past snowballed into... well, everything that happened."

Mike nodded, understanding in his eyes. "It's a sobering thought, isn't it? How the things we carry with us can shape our actions, even years later."

Sarah's mind flashed to her own past, the losses she'd endured, the walls she'd built. "Yeah," she said, her voice barely above a whisper. "It really is."

They stood in companionable silence for a moment, sipping their coffee and watching the city lights flicker in the distance.

"But you know what?" Sarah said suddenly, a spark of determination in her eyes. "I think... I think I'm ready to start dealing with my own baggage. Maybe it's time I talked to someone about... everything."

Mike smiled, genuine warmth in his expression. "I think that's a great idea, Sarah. You're one of the strongest people I know, but even the strongest need support sometimes."

As they turned to head back inside, Sarah felt a weight lift from her shoulders. The road ahead wouldn't be easy, but for the first time in a long while, she felt ready to face it head-on.

"Thanks, Mike," she said, her voice filled with quiet gratitude. "For everything."

The door closed behind them, but Sarah's heart felt more open than it had in years. She was ready for whatever came next, armed with a new understanding of the human heart and its complexities. And for now, that was enough.

Don't miss out!

Visit the website below and you can sign up to receive emails whenever Shane Reed publishes a new book. There's no charge and no obligation.

https://books2read.com/r/B-A-LSDAB-TZRFF

BOOKS2READ

Connecting independent readers to independent writers.

Did you love *Shadows of a Perfect Life*? Then you should read *The Sniffing Dog Scam*[1] by Shane Reed!

[2]

Suzie is an unassuming woman with a dark secret. With her canine companion, they were once hailed as heroes in the world of law enforcement for their uncanny ability to solve cold cases, their legacy takes a sinister turn as the truth behind their success is revealed.

Suzie and Charlie were renowned for their ability to unearth human remains, aiding in solving cases that had long gone cold. Their fame reached unprecedented heights as they assisted in high-profile assignments worldwide, even earning a feature on the popular TV show "Unsolved Mysteries."

Beneath the veneer of success lay a web of deception.

---

1. https://books2read.com/u/ba5Jnq

2. https://books2read.com/u/ba5Jnq

When Officer Tom James grows suspicious of Suzie's methods, a shocking revelation comes to light.

Based on a true story, this is a riveting exploration of the lengths one woman will go for fame and recognition, leaving a trail of desecrated remains and shattered trust in her wake.

Also by Shane Reed

A Conning Couple Novel
Checkmate
The Great Escape
The Queen's Gambit
The Sicilian Defense
Fool's Mate
The Scottish Game
Stale Mate
The Conning Couple Books 1-5

True Crime
The Sniffing Dog Scam
The Vengeful Parent
The Psychic Scam
Conterfeit Capitalist
Innocence On Trial
Voices Of Deception
Shadows of a Perfect Life

9 798227 841353